NECKLACE OF LIES

Book Two of the
Mizpah Ring Trilogy

DOROTHY STEWART

Zaccmedia

Published by Zaccmedia
www.zaccmedia.com
info@zaccmedia.com

Published November 2017

ISBN: 978-1-911211-67-9

British Library Cataloguing-in-Publication Data
A catalogue record for this book is available from the British Library.

ACKNOWLEDGEMENTS

Writing this book has given me great joy in revisiting many special places from my childhood. Thank you to my sister, Anna Rogalski, for accompanying me – and aiding and abetting me – as we scrambled through nettles and bracken, up and down rickety stairs, and poked our noses into fascinating places, all in the name of research!

Our day in Berriedale was very special. Thank you to Anson MacAuslan of Welbeck Estates (and Alexa) for all your help, Peter and Jenny Meredith at Langwell Gardens, George Mathieson whose guided tour of the sawmill furnished much useful material for the book, Mr and Mrs Frances Higginson who showed us round the old Smiddy where we stayed so often with our grandparents, and Paul Kerridge and Barbara Clements for opening up the Portland Hall for us to look around.

During that trip north, I was privileged to give a talk to a meeting of the Caithness Family History Society and benefited from a wealth of World War II memories from the members. Thank you! Invaluable too was the 'Wings over Wick' series of memories of Wick during the war from members of the Air Force, collected by Primary 7, Hillhead

School, Wick, and published in 1993. I found this treasure trove on www.Caithness.org/wings/index.htm.

Thank you also to Hazel Stewart at the National Library of Scotland who pointed me in the direction of Denise Davie at the Mitchell Library, Glasgow, who located and sent me photocopies of the series of nine articles 'A Scot in Chicago's Gangland' written by an ex-gangster, James Gilzean, and published in the *Weekly Record* in 1930. And thank you to Carol-Anne Mackenzie at Wick Library Family History Centre who found me the editions of the *John O'Groat Journal* I needed to check.

Three books which provided much background information were:

City of Gangs: Glasgow and the Rise of the British Gangster by Andrew Davies, Hodder & Stoughton, 2013

Caithness and the War, 1939-1945 by N. M. Glass, North of Scotland Newspapers, 1994

The 'Sawdust Fusiliers': The Canadian Forestry Corps in the Scottish Highlands in World War Two by William C. Wonders, Canadian Pulp and Paper Association, 1991

At school, 'history' finished at the end of the First World War so I was surprised – amazed and shocked, as well as proud – to discover the part my home town played in this conflict – and how much it suffered. I have aimed for accuracy in the telling of my fictional story and I hope I have honoured all those who were involved and who lost loved ones, or were affected.

Grateful thanks are due to the Wick Society for permission to use the photographs from the Johnston Collection on the cover, and especially to Fergus Mather for his help.

And as always, a big vote of thanks to Paul Stanier, my publisher at Zaccmedia and cover-design genius, and my eagle-eyed editor Mollie Barker. Two down, one to go!

CHAPTER 1

Wick, Caithness, Scotland, 1938

Joyce Cormack methodically folded the last letter from the pile on her desk and slid it into an envelope. She licked the gum and sealed the flap.

'There!' she said, with satisfaction. 'All done.' She squared up the teetering pile of letters now ready for the post and stacked them tidily in her out-tray.

The young woman at the desk facing her – a peroxide blonde with bright red lipstick – was buffing her nails, a bored expression on her face. The movie magazine she had been flicking through lay open on the desk in front of her.

'Don't you ever wish for more out of life?' she asked Joyce, her pretty face marred by discontent. 'Something more exciting than this?' She waved her hand round the office they shared.

Joyce's steady brown eyes followed Ruby's dismissive gesture. She saw freshly cream-emulsioned walls, a cheerful fire crackling in the grate, the two desks with their typewriters and filing trays. Across the room a sliding glass partition above a wooden counter separated them from the tiny outer office with its front door into the street, and kept them private and cosy.

'I don't see anything wrong with this,' Joyce said. 'Honestly, we're a lot better off than many. When Dad bought the garage and the house, he spent good money on converting this room into an office and making it all modern and comfortable for us.'

Ruby's face set into a sulk. 'You would say that,' she complained. 'You're the Boss's daughter.'

'Well, I can't do anything about that!' Joyce laughed. 'But still, I genuinely like it here. I know you think it's boring of me but I like being next door to Mum in the house on this side.' She gestured to the door beside her which led into the adjoining house. 'And having Dad and Bobby in the garage on the other.'

Ruby raised her carefully pencilled eyebrows in exasperation. 'But don't you ever want to get away from them? Have a life of your own? See the world? Meet different people?'

But Joyce smilingly shook her head.

'No, I don't. I like being here with my family. I think I'm really blessed that I can work in the family business and not have to find a job somewhere else. And I enjoy the work. I find it interesting. I love seeing all the different people who come in wanting to hire cars. We hear about weddings, often before anyone else in town...'

'And funerals,' Ruby put in snappily. 'And accidents...'

It was true that the Cormack Car Hire Company supplied hearses and ambulances as well as smart cars for weddings. Joyce's lips quirked with amusement. She knew she was simply going over old ground with Ruby. When the other girl was bored or unhappy, she invariably launched into this litany of discontent.

Joyce watched her pick up the movie magazine then fling it away from her irritably.

'So what's the matter?' Joyce coaxed her. 'You won't have to work here much longer. Once you're married to Bobby, with your own home...'

But Ruby was not going to be comforted. She turned the engagement ring round on her finger and glared at it.

'He doesn't seem to be in any hurry to get married.' She glanced up at Joyce, suddenly cross. 'What is it with you Cormacks? No get up and go!'

'Is that what you really want?' Joyce asked in surprise. 'For Bobby to be dynamic and in a hurry to go places?' She considered the gentle steady nature of her beloved half-brother. 'That wouldn't be Bobby at all.' Her brow furrowed. 'If that's what you want, you'll need to find someone else.' She gasped as the words came out of her mouth. 'I didn't mean that! You wouldn't do that, would you? It would break his heart!'

Ruby smiled craftily. 'It might not hurt him! Just to worry him a bit, see if he'd get a move on! I'm not getting any younger...'

'You're only two years older than me,' Joyce protested. 'And I'm in no hurry to get married!'

'Maybe, but I feel a lot older,' Ruby said. 'And time won't stand still just because Bobby's not in a hurry either. I'll be in my dotage before we're married!'

Joyce laughed. 'Silly!' she said. 'Shall I make us a cup of tea?'

Ruby reached for her magazine just as the outer door opened. Through the dividing glass partition, the girls could see a man, a smartly dressed stranger, approaching the counter.

'You go,' Joyce told Ruby in a low voice. 'Maybe this is your bit of excitement for today!' She giggled.

Ruby glared at her and pointedly raised the magazine.

3

'Oh, all right,' Joyce said with resignation. 'I'll deal with him.'
She stood up and slid open the window above the counter.
'Good afternoon,' she said politely. 'How may I help you?'

CHAPTER 2

Velvety dark-brown eyes captured hers and Joyce felt as if she were falling into their depths as their owner smiled bewitchingly at her. His voice was foreign and melodious, caressing her senses. Realising he had asked a question, Joyce had to use all her willpower to drag her attention back to business.

'I'm terribly sorry,' she said, a hot blush flooding her cheeks. 'What did you say?'

'Ah, it is I who should be sorry!' the man said in that beautiful voice. 'I still do not speak English perfectly!' But his smile told her he was teasing. He knew she had been bewitched.

'No, no, your English is perfectly fine,' Joyce said, shaking her head in denial. 'What was it you wanted?'

He sighed, as if he were unwilling to drag his attention from the pleasures of conversation with her to matters of business.

'A car,' he said simply. 'I should like to hire a car – and a driver,' he added.

He shrugged and waved a hand. Joyce stared in sudden fascination. His skin was smooth and tanned, and his nails were clean and perfectly shaped – so very different from the men she was used to. Her father and half-brother Bobby had rough-skinned hands stained with engine oil and grease, nails broken and bluntly clipped. The young farmers she had been out with had rough work-soiled hands too.

But this man's hands were those of a gentleman. That was plain to see.

'I myself drive, of course,' he was saying. 'At home...'

'And where might that be?' Ruby had pushed in beside Joyce and was now leaning her elbows on the counter observing the newcomer with pert interest.

The man's smile included Ruby as he answered, 'Buenos Aires. In Argentina.' He gave the girls a courtly little bow. 'I am George St Clair at your service.' He smiled again, his teeth white against his tanned skin, as he added, 'My real name is Jorge.' The word sounded like *Horrhay*. 'But people in this country find it too difficult to pronounce so I use the English version, George.'

The girls exchanged delighted glances and Joyce nudged Ruby surreptitiously. This exotic stranger was definitely providing a bit of Ruby's longed-for excitement.

He was watching them, waiting, and Joyce forced herself into business-like speech.

'You said you wanted a car, Mr St Clair?'

'Ah yes. And a driver.' Again that devastatingly attractive smile. 'I shall be here for a few days – I have family business to attend to. But I should like to spend what time I can seeing the country, the land of my father.'

'Oh, your folks came from here?' Ruby asked, leaning forward and edging Joyce to the side.

'My father came from this area originally,' George St Clair said. 'My mother is Argentinian.'

The girls nodded. *That would explain his beautiful tan and his lovely manners,* Joyce thought.

'I have my mother's family name as my middle name,' George St Clair said. 'De la Vega.'

Joyce ran the name silently over in her mind: George de la Vega St Clair. It was as romantically beautiful as the man standing in front of her in his elegantly tailored suit, expensive shirt, and perfectly groomed hands. De la Vega St Clair. And suddenly she found herself like a schoolgirl trying out the name along with hers: Joyce de la Vega St Clair... It sounded wonderful. And so right. Her heart leapt. It sounded so amazingly right.

She jumped as Ruby pushed her aside and grabbed the appointments book.

'Let me see,' Ruby said, opening it up. 'When would you like the car to take you out?'

'Tomorrow?' George St Clair gave that expressive continental shrug.

Joyce could feel Ruby give a little shiver in response, before she looked down at the book.

'Tomorrow?' she repeated. 'Mmm, yes, I think we could do that. Starting at about ten?'

Joyce edged in to look.

'Yes.' She pointed at the page. 'My brother Bobby will be your driver. Just tell him what you'd like to see, where you'd like to go, and he'll look after you.'

George St Clair bowed again and smiled. And in that moment Joyce felt that his smile was for her alone as his dark eyes locked onto hers. She felt her heart pound and realised she was barely breathing.

'Ladies,' he said. 'I shall see you tomorrow morning.'

And putting his soft dark hat on his glossy black hair, he turned and left the office, closing the door behind him.

'Well!' Ruby said, turning back to her desk. 'He was certainly something!'

Joyce smiled dreamily. 'And we'll see him again tomorrow,' she said.

CHAPTER 3

The Cormack family were enjoying their evening meal, sitting round the big circular table in the dining room. There was a warm fire blazing in the hearth, and they were chatting cheerfully, sharing the news of the day. Second son of the family, Danny, who worked at the local weekly newspaper *The Caithness Sentinel*, had brought them up to date on various snippets of interest, but the most exciting topic came from his sister Joyce and their half-brother Bobby.

'How was your day out with Mr St Clair?' Joyce had asked Bobby. 'I want to hear all about it!'

'Oh ho!' Bobby grinned. 'She's in love again!' He laughed as Joyce blushed and glared crossly at him.

'He's interesting and I like him,' she said with an attempt at dignity. 'That's all.'

Danny groaned. 'Oh, not again. Tell all,' he instructed. 'Who is this Mr St Clair?'

'A stranger to the town!' Bobby teased. 'A tall, dark and handsome stranger.'

'Well, that figures,' Danny agreed. 'One look and...'

'Now, now,' his father chided him gently.

Rab Cormack leaned back in his chair and surveyed his three children. They had turned out fine, even if the boys did have a tendency to tease their younger sister. Boys, he caught himself with a wry smile. They were men now. Bobby, his son by his ill-fated first marriage, was now thirty-seven years old, and his right-hand man in the business. Danny at twenty-five was well-settled in his chosen career. He had served his apprenticeship as a typesetter and printer and was now a respected member of the staff that turned out the weekly broadsheet. His sister, Joyce, was the baby of the family. A very special blessing that crowned the love he had discovered in his marriage to her mother. Joyce's gentle steady nature was a boon both in the business and in the good-natured way she generally dealt with her brothers.

Her mother... Rab smiled across the table at his beloved Hannah. She would want to know all the details about this stranger who had apparently captivated their daughter. He turned to Bobby.

'You're talking about that foreign man you took out today?'

'Yes.' Bobby twinkled at his half-sister. 'And Joyce is in love with him already! Met him only the once...'

'Twice,' Joyce muttered rebelliously.

'Oh yes.' Bobby acknowledged the correction. 'First, when he booked the hire, and the second time when he came in this morning before we went out. Must have been all of...' He gazed at the ceiling as if thinking hard. 'Ten minutes? Five?'

'Don't tease your sister,' his father repeated automatically, then catching his wife's eye added, 'Tell us what you know about this man.'

'Well, he's called St Clair. Not Sinclair.' Bobby enunciated the names, clearly demonstrating the differences in pronunciation: *Saint Clair*, the emphasis evenly between the two words; *Sinkler* with the emphasis on the first syllable. 'Jorge St Clair.' He struggled with the pronunciation. 'It's Spanish. He's from Buenos Aires, in the Argentine.'

'And?' his father prompted.

'Seems perfectly nice…' Bobby said.

'He's a gentleman,' Joyce said fiercely. 'Anyone can see that!'

Hannah Cormack exchanged a tolerant smile with her husband across the table.

'Handsome is as handsome does, my love,' she cautioned Joyce gently.

At eighteen, their only daughter had all the fire and enthusiasm of youth, especially towards what was new and exciting. And Hannah had to admit that Jorge St Clair was certainly new and his arrival in the quiet little town of Wick had created quite a stir of excitement.

'Anyway,' Hannah added as a further gentle damper, 'he's probably only here for a short visit.'

'Yes, I think that's probably right,' Bobby said. 'I don't think he was that impressed with Caithness.'

'Why do you think that?' Hannah asked her stepson.

'Well,' he said thoughtfully, 'he seemed keen enough when we set off, leaning forward and looking at everything, asking questions. I drove him out towards John O'Groats but after a while he seemed to lose interest.' Bobby paused. 'He said, "We also have sheep farms in my country – but they are big, thousands of acres, not scrappy little peasant farms on poor land like these." Then he said, "Is there nowhere more interesting?" So I took him down the coast so he could see the sea views and Dunbeath Castle. That seemed more the kind of thing he was interested in.'

'The views or the castle?' his father asked dryly.

'Oh, the castle,' Bobby said. 'He liked that fine.' He added, 'He's come north on family business, he said. I think he's going to come into some money and was maybe looking to see what he could spend it on.'

'He's rich already, though,' Joyce put in.

Her family turned questioning eyes on her.

'Well...' She waved her hand. 'You can see – his clothes, his hands...'

'Oh, there's no shortage of money,' Bobby agreed. He pushed his still-laden plate away from him. 'He bought me a slap-up meal at the Portland Arms on our way back through Lybster. Sorry, Mum. I'm just not so hungry tonight.'

Hannah rose to clear the plates.

'Joyce.' She nudged her daughter but Joyce was lost in her daydreams. So George had money and was going to come into more. He was looking to buy in Caithness, to settle here. Maybe in a castle.

She ran the lovely daydream name through her head again: Joyce de la Vega St Clair. Living in a castle with the handsome George de la Vega St Clair...

'Joyce!'

Her mother's voice, firmer now, broke through her dreams. Joyce blinked. She realised her family was staring at her, amusement mingled with affection. Her father shook his head but he was smiling. Blushing, Joyce rose to help her mother.

CHAPTER 4

'George St Clair.'

George presented his card with a bow, noting the delighted squirm of the plain, rather plump young woman behind the reception desk in the solicitor's office. He smiled confidently.

'I have an appointment with Mr Aitchison,' he said.

George had discovered from his driver that Aitchisons was the firm that dealt with the landed gentry and the large estates round here. Clearly they were the right people for him to deal with so he had wasted no time in making an appointment to see the senior solicitor.

The girl took his card through to a room across the hall, and after a few moments George was shown into a comfortably appointed office. Dark wood bookshelves filled with leather-bound tomes lined one wall. Overflowing files tied with pink ribbon were piled in untidy heaps on the richly hued carpet. George smiled with satisfaction. The room gave all the signs of belonging to a busy and successful solicitor.

'Mr Aitchison, Mr St Clair,' the girl announced, then with a decidedly flirtatious glance at George, left them.

Behind a huge dark wood desk sat an elderly gentleman in a pinstripe suit. He peered over gold-rimmed glasses at George.

'Mr St Clair?' he said. 'We call it Sinclair up here.' And the man spelled it, carefully. 'S-I-N-C-L-A-I-R.'

George waved it away. 'St Clair. Sinclair. What difference does it make?' He shrugged and stepped across the room uninvited to claim the leather chair in front of the desk. Throwing himself into it, he announced, 'I am here to discover my father's people and to claim my inheritance. I believe there is a castle and some land... And I am the only son...'

He paused, holding his eagerness in check.

Mr Aitchison's eyes narrowed. Folding his hands together on the gilt-edged leather-bound blotter on his desk, the elderly solicitor leaned forward and repeated, 'Castle?'

George nodded.

'Is that so?' the solicitor asked thoughtfully. 'And would you know which one?'

'Yes, of course,' George said confidently. 'It carries the family name. St Clair Castle.'

A strange spasm crossed the solicitor's face. His eyes seemed to bulge. He swallowed hard.

'I see. As I said, up here we say Sinclair not St Clair, so – let me just get this right – would that be "Castle Sinclair" as in "Sinclair and Girnigoe"? You see,' he explained, 'they go together.'

George racked his brains. Was that what his mother had said? He could not quite remember. There had been so many stories. Sofia Maria de la Vega St Clair had been widowed tragically early. George, only a baby less than a year old at the time, had no actual memory of his father. After his death, his maternal grandparents – the de la Vegas – had sent them out to the family estancia on the pampas

14

so Sofia Maria could recover from her bereavement in peace and privacy.

As George grew and was able to understand that his father was dead, he had plagued his mother for stories about him. And she had told him such wonderful things. He had realised, with joy, that his father had been an important man in his own country.

'Scotland,' his mother had explained. 'Somewhere in the far north.'

His father's homeland was in the county of Caithness, he had discovered. From an early age, it had been his dream to go to Scotland and see where his father had grown up – and now he was here.

His mother had told him stories of great estates and shooting parties with the English Royal Family. And castles. Yes, he remembered St Clair Castle, of course, clearly the family one, but what about the other one the solicitor had mentioned? Girnigoe? George's memory was not clear about it. He had been very young and the memories were misty.

But surely two castles were much better than one?

'Yes,' George declared confidently. 'That would be it.'

At which the old man appeared to have a seizure. His face turned purple, his eyes flooded with tears, and a strange wheezing sound came out of his mouth.

George watched in bewilderment. After a few moments, the solicitor appeared to recover. He wiped his eyes and seemed to pull himself together.

'Oh dearie me,' he said, replacing the gold-rimmed spectacles on his nose. 'That's the best laugh I've had in many, many years!'

'*Laugh?*' George stared at him, sudden rage rising in him. *No one laughed at George St Clair.*

'You will tell me what you find so funny, *señor*,' he ground out. 'I do not see...'

Mr Aitchison flapped a hand at him. 'Well, you wouldn't,' he agreed easily. 'Coming from as far away as you do. Oh dear me,' and his shoulders began to shake again.

George rose and leaned over the desk. 'I will ask you one more time...' But his icy tones seemed to have no effect.

The solicitor simply shook his head, once more wiped his eyes, and said, 'I will explain. I will explain.' He paused a moment to collect his thoughts, then called, 'Jessie!'

The secretary who had shown George into the solicitor's presence came to the door.

'Yes, Mr Aitchison?'

'Jessie, can you find me a picture of Sinclair and Girnigoe Castle? In a book, or on a postcard? As soon as you can, if you please.'

'Yes, Mr Aitchison, right away. I think there may be a book...' Her voice trailed away as she exited the room, her round face a picture of curiosity.

'I think it would be best if I showed you, so you can see for yourself,' the solicitor said. 'And while we're waiting, perhaps you'd like to tell me a little about yourself?'

George settled back into his chair reassured. There would be an explanation. There was nothing to worry about. He smiled, showing large white teeth, and began a well-practised spiel.

'As I have said, I am George St Clair, *señor*,' he said. 'From Buenos Aires. In Spanish my name is *Jorge*, but people who do not speak the language find it too difficult to say.' He waved a hand as in a negligent assumption of mutual understanding. 'I therefore use the English version.'

The old solicitor nodded.

'My father, after whom I am named,' George continued, 'was George St Clair. He came of a landed family from this county and had much wealth. A man of far-sighted enterprise, he went to the Klondike during the days of the Gold Rush and made a second fortune there.'

'The Klondike?' the solicitor murmured thoughtfully. 'Is that so? George St Clair...' He repeated the name. 'George St Clair. Mmm. I wonder...'

'The gold mine was left in the hands of managers and he moved to San Francisco where he had many business interests.'

He slowed here. Try as he might, George had never been able to discover what those interests had been and though he had spent some time in San Francisco there had been no trace to be found. This had been a major setback in tracking down his father's fortune, especially after the discovery that when the Gold Rush in the Klondike had decisively ended all the original mines had closed.

'Indeed,' the solicitor said, steepling his fingers as he listened attentively.

'Indeed,' George asserted, and continued the story he remembered his mother telling him. 'He met my uncle, Federico de la Vega, in San Francisco. My uncle was young and had got into some kind of trouble but my papa paid for him to return to Buenos Aires – and accompanied him. There, he met my mama, and the rest as they say' – George shrugged his expensively tailored shoulders – 'is history!'

At that moment, Jessie the secretary returned and was rewarded by George with a welcoming smile. The girl blushed an uncomfortable brick red and, having placed a book with a paper place mark in it on the solicitor's desk, scuttled out of the room.

George smiled and leaned forward eagerly, but Mr Aitchison was in no hurry.

'And yourself, Mr St Clair? What is your history?'

George shifted in his seat. He had expected the arrival of the book to prevent him having to account for his life so far.

'Myself?' he asked, aiming for a careless tone. 'My history is not so interesting.'

'Come now,' the solicitor encouraged him. 'It is not every day I get the chance to meet a young man from so far away. Please, humour an old man!'

George considered. After a moment he said in a light-hearted voice, 'It's the usual – I was brought up in Argentina and went to school there. After my father's death my mother remarried and went to live on her new husband's estancia.'

Carefully he kept the bitterness out of his voice. Sofia Maria's marriage to Ramon Hernandez had marked a sea-change in his life. Suddenly George had to share his mother not only with a husband but an increasing family of siblings: Federico, named after his mother's brother, Carolina, Ronaldo, and little Catalena. George hauled his mind back to his story.

'Ramon is a cattle rancher and involved in meat processing. It is a lucrative business. After I left school, he took me into the business and later I was sent to America – to Chicago – to look after that side of the business.'

There was no need to tell this old man that he had been sent to school because of trouble at home, that he had then been expelled from school and sent to America as a bribe to keep him out of further trouble. George took a steadying breath.

'I was there for a while.'

He smiled, recalling his years in Chicago when bootlegging was much more interesting – and lucrative – than meat processing. Though the ensuing jail sentence had not been such a good experience. His

Scottish antecedents, however, had won him deportation to Glasgow with the other Scottish henchmen of the Chicago gangsters. There then followed the years with them in Scotland – at first so promising, then as the police cracked down on the Glasgow gangs, life had turned sour once more – but there was no need to mention any of that either.

'I grew older and began to think of settling down, marriage even.' Again that shrug, an appeal for understanding between men. 'I felt it was time to discover my roots, my father's people.'

It had certainly been time to get out of Glasgow and hopefully discover a legacy worth coming all this way for.

'And so here I am.'

He raised his hands in a charming gesture, inviting the solicitor to smile with him.

George settled back into his chair with a satisfied smile. The stitched-together story had flowed seamlessly. It all appeared eminently respectable – no mention of gangsters and guns, either in Chicago or Glasgow. But the word 'respectable' suddenly pricked him. Would inheriting the family castle force him into living a staid, respectable life? It suddenly felt suffocatingly boring.

The sight of the solicitor opening the book halted that thought in its tracks. The man had mentioned *two* castles! There had to be real wealth involved. Now that would not be boring!

The solicitor pressed the open book flat, his hands covering the photographs George was anxious to see. He looked up at George.

'I think this is what we were looking for,' he said. 'Castle Sinclair and Girnigoe.' And with a flourish he swung the book round towards George.

CHAPTER 5

George stared at the photograph. It showed two castles. On a jutting headland of rock above a stormy sea.

Two castles. Yes. But...

He looked up at the elderly solicitor.

'*This?*' George asked. '*These* are Sinclair and Girnigoe Castles? *My* castles?' And what he saw in answer was a kind of pity in the old man's eyes.

'*This* is Castle Sinclair and Girnigoe,' Mr Aitchison said. 'Just as you see.' He gestured to the clear black-and-white image of the ruins on the rocky headland. 'It's been like this since around 1700.'

'*1700?*' George swallowed hard. No new, unexpected dilapidation then. These castles had been like this for hundreds of years. *Ruins.* He felt the fury build in him. He had come all this way just for ruins!

But the solicitor was continuing: 'And I'm afraid they are not *your* castles. They belong to a local landowner, Sir George of the Duff-Dunbar family, and have done for generations.'

George pushed the book away from him and sat down heavily. Mr Aitchison continued to gaze sorrowfully at him.

'Is there more?' George ground out.

The man chewed his lip. 'I don't know where you got your information…' he began.

'My sainted mama,' George said with a bitter laugh, recalling the memories he had clung to, the pictures and the stories fed to him by his adoring mother. He paused as he thought now: his adoring mother – before that *péon* Ramon Hernandez had spoiled everything…

The solicitor gave him a disapproving glance. 'She may have been, but your father was not. I'm sorry.' Mr Aitchison looked over his gold-rimmed spectacles at George. 'I'm afraid, despite what you may have been told, your father did not belong to the county's elite. In fact, rather the opposite.'

George hissed his fury at the insult, but the old solicitor held up a hand to hold him back.

'I remember your father,' he said.

George stared. 'You knew my father?' At last, someone with a real connection to him.

Mr Aitchison's lip curled. 'I wouldn't go so far as to say I *knew* him.' With a disparaging smile, he added, 'We didn't exactly move in the same circles, you understand. But I certainly knew enough *of* him, and about him.'

'Tell me,' George ground out. It surely could not get any worse.

'Are you sure you want to know?' Again, the solicitor's eyes seemed to convey pity.

George waved it away. He had no need of pity.

'Just tell me what you know,' he spat out.

'All right,' Mr Aitchison said. He steepled his fingers together once more and drew a long breath before he spoke in magisterial tones. 'When your father lived in Wick, he was known as Geordie Sinclair and he was one of the town's ne'er-do-wells.'

George's dark eyes flashed with anger.

The solicitor continued inexorably, 'Yes, it is true that he went out to the Klondike and he may have found gold there.'

George nodded, his fury somewhat assuaged. So some at least of his mother's story was true. Perhaps there was hope...

'But he had neither land nor castle here,' the solicitor stated. 'Geordie Sinclair came from a wretched hovel in the poorest part of town, and the company he kept was of the worst type. His family belonged to the criminal orders.'

George felt unwilling laughter rising up in him. His father's family belonged to the criminal orders and he had been worrying about having to take on a mantle of boring respectability! He thought back to his own years with the Capone gang in Chicago, with Scots Jimmy and his friends in Glasgow. How could this information about his father – his forebears – possibly come as a surprise? How could he ever have been expected to take after the oh-so-proud and respectable de la Vega family? He would never have fitted in to his mother's new life with her ultra-respectable husband and those so dutiful and well-behaved Hernandez children! All these years, he had indeed been a cuckoo in the nest.

He had come all this way for his inheritance – castle, lands, wealth – and instead of discovering that he belonged to the landed elite, with a new life of moneyed ease ahead of him, he had indeed come into his inheritance – his true inheritance – as he discovered who he really was – whose son he had been all along. And now he saw clearly whose *true* son he was, for surely he had followed unknowingly in his father's footsteps from the very start.

He realised the old solicitor was still talking.

'I would not recommend that you make their acquaintance. Not if you want to maintain any respectability in this town.'

Make the acquaintance of his father's family? His true family? The solicitor's disdainful advice lit a sudden strong flare of rebellion. Yes, of course he would do just that. What did he care about respectability? It was too late for that.

He would search out his relatives and get the true story of his father's life, and then he would decide exactly what he was going to do with his life.

Mr Aitchison stood up.

'I am sorry. This is not the news you were expecting.'

'That is true,' George said, his thoughts racing. How was he going to contact his family? He knew it would not be wise to ask the solicitor. But in a town this small, surely it would not be difficult? And surely they would be pleased to welcome home his father's son?

He stood up, and turned to leave. Behind him, the solicitor's eyes narrowed in disapproval.

'Jessie,' the man called out.

The plump secretary's head appeared at the door.

'Make sure Mr Sinclair...' He stressed the local pronunciation of the name. No more Mr St Clair, George noted. 'Make sure he has a note of what he owes us before he goes.' Mr Aitchison nodded abruptly at George. 'And that he pays it.'

He remained standing, waiting for George to leave.

George paused, fury in his eyes at the open insult. So he was no longer the rich Argentinian gentleman worthy of courtesy. Now he was simply the offspring of one of the town's black sheep – and probably a black sheep in his own right, not to be trusted with the payment of a little bill.

23

George's lip curled. Little did this Aitchison know how right he was! His black eyes flashed. Well, his father had got away from this sanctimonious little town and he *had* made his fortune. George squared his shoulders. He was his father's true son and he would show them! He was not finished with them yet!

CHAPTER 6

Outside the solicitor's office George lingered for a moment on the pavement as he considered his options. First he needed a drink. He could return to his hotel and get a drink at the bar there, but what he needed most of all was information about his father's family and how to reach them – and that information was unlikely to be found there.

He had been amazed to discover on his arrival in Wick that the town was dry – echoing the Prohibition-era Chicago he had left so recently. There were few legitimate places to drink – and if he was going to find out the true story of his antecedents, he would need to find one of the illegal drinking places that would be frequented by the kind of folk who would know. The kind of folk who might have known his father.

But how was he going to find such a place? The car and driver had been returned to the garage where his payment had been accepted by the pretty dark-haired child in the office. It was unlikely any of the folks there would help him. They seemed very – he sneered at the very word – respectable. But there had been the bold-eyed blonde beside her who had clearly found him of interest and perhaps did not share this town's obsession with respectability. But how to engineer contact? He did not want to hire a car again. He was not sure his remaining funds would stretch to it. He had pinned all his hopes on his inheritance – and being able to get a cash advance on it.

The rage rose again in him as he remembered the supercilious solicitor's pity as he showed him the picture of the castle ruins. He wanted to smash…

Firmly George dismissed the impulse and slowly turned his steps back towards the hotel. At least he would get a drink there.

'Mr St Clair! Fancy bumping into you!'

The female voice was loud, local, and cheerful. Blue eyes sparkled in a rosy face framed with unashamedly peroxided hair. It was the blonde from the car hire company, dressed today in fashionable street-clothes, the tight waist and short skirt defining a curvaceous figure.

'A coincidence indeed,' George agreed with a smile, as he wondered how much of a coincidence it really was. This young woman knew what she was about. 'Are you not working today, perhaps?'

She smiled broadly. 'I have the rest of the day off. And what about you? Are you busy or would you like some company?'

Her boldness pleased him.

'I would indeed welcome some company,' he told her, and offered his arm which she took with alacrity.

'Would you like to do some sightseeing?' she asked brightly. 'There's not that much to see…'

'Oh, I don't know,' George said, looking at her appreciatively.

The girl grinned at the unspoken compliment and tossed her waved blonde head. George grinned back. He congratulated himself. It appeared that lucky Georgie had landed on his feet again. This was definitely his kind of girl. But first things first.

'What I want is a drink,' George stated. 'But not in there.' He waved at the nearby hotel.

'There are other hotels,' the girl offered.

'No,' George said firmly. 'I want somewhere...'

She was staring at him in puzzlement.

'Somewhere with a bit more atmosphere,' he concluded.

'Atmosphere?' she echoed.

'Local colour,' George prompted.

Ruby grimaced. 'Well, there are one or two dives...' She hesitated, adding, 'You know the town's dry so they're not exactly legal... Not the place for a visitor.'

'I shall be the judge of that,' George stated. 'Now take me to one of them, whichever you like. You choose.'

'They're not very respectable places,' Ruby said. 'You'd do better at the hotel or...' She paused, considering. 'I'm sure I could offer you some refreshment at my place,' she offered.

George laughed. 'That sounds very nice. Maybe we can go to your place later.'

The smile the girl gave him told him she understood the unspoken message and was not offended.

'But I want a drink *now*,' George continued. 'And as to how respectable the place is – well, maybe I'm not very respectable either. Now, be a good girl and lead on.'

Ruby shrugged and pulled his arm gently to turn him away from the solicitor's office, just as the door opened and Jessie, Mr Aitchison's secretary, came out. She stared at them, pointedly focusing on Ruby's arm entwined in George's.

'I wouldn't waste your time on him, Ruby Mowat,' she said contemptuously. 'Mr St Clair...' She emphasised the name sarcastically. 'Mr St Clair has just discovered everything there is to know about his family castles and his inheritance!' She tittered derisively. 'Bit of a surprise, wasn't it?'

George felt the anger surge within him, but to his surprise, Ruby squeezed his arm quellingly.

'Really?' Ruby asked the girl, her thin pencilled eyebrows rising in a coldly repressive glare.

'Aye, and you needn't come the fine lady with me. You're not much better yourself!' Jessie said. She waved at George. 'This one thought he was about to inherit Sinclair and Girnigoe Castle, would you believe?' And she burst into mocking laughter. 'Can you imagine?'

'Sinclair and Girnigoe?' Ruby repeated. She flung a quick questioning look at George.

'Yes!' Jessie crowed triumphantly. 'He came all this way for his inheritance... Him that's only the son of Geordie Sinclair that was, not some fine landed gentry!' And she turned and marched up the street, her plump shoulders heaving with laughter.

Ruby turned to George, her eyes fixed on his.

'Is this true?' she asked quietly.

'It would appear so,' he replied. He waited to see her reaction, surprised to discover that it mattered.

'Oh well,' she said with a sudden grin. 'If that's what you've just found out, I can see why you would need a drink so bad. Come on then! I know exactly the right place!'

And she led him away.

CHAPTER 7

Ruby had described it accurately. It was a dive and not a place to take an innocent tourist. But to one who had frequented all manner of speakeasies in Chicago, it had the familiarity of home.

The girl knocked, a pattern of raps, then when the door opened a crack, she whispered some words in her strange harsh dialect. They seemed to do the trick. The crack opened wider and from the darkness within appeared a swarthy face with bloodshot eyes which examined George. The man spoke again to Ruby, clearly questioning her. And she, angrily now, appeared to be arguing back.

Finally the door was opened, grudgingly, and they were allowed into a dark and smoky room. A fire smouldered in a hearth, and in the room's low light George could just make out small groups hunched over drinks, or slouched in their chairs. A makeshift bar was set against the back wall.

'This your kind of place?' she asked with amusement.

George reacted without thinking. The slap was audible but, to his surprise, the girl did not cower away from him. Instead she stepped forward and, without hesitation, slapped him back. Hard.

'This isn't your fine Buenos Aires here, Mr St Clair!' she told him, breathless with anger. 'We're on my home turf and I'm not one of your fine little *señoritas* – so don't you forget it! Now, do you want that drink? Or maybe we should be getting out of here before my friends take exception to your manners!'

She glanced round the room. All eyes were fixed on them. Some of the men were clearly poised to take action if necessary.

George raised both hands in surrender and began to laugh.

'Thank you, my dear, for that demonstration,' he said smoothly. 'You are clearly worth a thousand of the fine little *señoritas*!'

Ruby's eyes narrowed.

'I'll get those drinks,' she said and stalked away to the back of the room.

George sat down at a table from where he could watch proceedings. He could hear Ruby talking. At last, the man she was speaking to picked up a bottle and two tumblers and brought them over to the table. He set them down, staring hard at George.

'Just who are you?' the man demanded. 'And what do you want?'

'I want information,' George said in a clear carrying tone so everyone in the room could hear him. 'I want to know about my father...' He looked round the bar, trying to see into the gloom. 'It is possible some of you may remember him. He came from here.'

That started up a murmur of voices.

'A Weeker?' came the question.

The girl, back at his side, translated for his benefit. 'From Wick? Your father came from Wick?'

'That is so.' George waited.

'And his name?'

George waited till the hubbub died down.

'George St Clair.' He added the local pronunciation. 'Sinclair.' Then he spoke the name his mother had always used, the name the old solicitor had used: 'Geordie.'

'Geordie St Clair. Geordie Sinclair...'

The name echoed around the smoky room. Then there were nudges and glances.

'You're Geordie Sinclair's son?' the bartender asked.

'Yes,' George said. 'I am.'

As he said it, it felt like a last throw of the dice, the last card in the game. But he had nothing left to play. He stilled himself to wait.

The man poured a generous slug of the straw-coloured liquid into each glass. He handed one to Geordie and took the other himself. He raised his glass in salute.

'Welcome home!' he said ironically. 'Ruby, go and get yourself another glass. Now, how can we help you, Mr Sinclair...'

'George. After my father.'

The glass was raised in his direction again.

'George. Welcome home. Now what can we do for you?'

CHAPTER 8

'So that's the last we heard of him,' one of the older men finished his story. Interspersed with comments and details from many of the folk present, it had taken a while.

Geordie may have been a ne'er-do-well to the self-righteous solicitor, Mr Aitchison, but it was clear that in this environment he was a kind of folk hero. When he lived in Wick, he had been one of the youthful leaders of the criminal fraternity. George had listened with some satisfaction. His father's brushes with the law had all been small-time compared with his own exploits in Chicago.

'So now you know,' another man who had provided many of the details said.

A white-haired old man in a fisherman's navy jersey added, 'This is where your roots are and we're your people.' He raised his glass and toasted George. 'You're welcome here!'

'Your turn now,' the shebeen owner said. 'Tell us what happened to Geordie.'

Avid faces turned to George. He sifted carefully through the possibilities. There was Mama's story of the handsome, wealthy Scotsman with his land and his castle and his Klondike gold. That seemed more and more like a fairytale. A deliberate fabrication even, George thought, in the light of what he was learning.

It appeared that his father had been a con-man. A petty criminal from this remote part of Scotland, living on his wits in a foreign land. First there had been the Klondike venture – and George had been unable to identify any gold mine or claim in his father's name, though he was sure his father had got to the Klondike. Then there were the San Francisco business interests. Again, he had drawn a blank when he had visited San Francisco, but he knew for a fact that his father had been in San Francisco when he met Uncle Federico. Had all the stories simply been carefully spun fantasies to win Geordie entrance into the wealthy de la Vega family?

The once-wealthy de la Vega family, George corrected himself. There had been enough money for his grandfather to pay the gambling debts his father had left behind when he was killed, but that had all but wiped out the family fortune.

Geordie's end had been an embarrassment to the respectable de la Vega family. Shot in a poker game. Accused of cheating. Everything was covered up, hushed up. No one would speak of it. It was only later, as George grew up, that he had begun to piece together the facts. As a young lad, he had thought it tragic and romantic. But now?

His eyes focused back on the people around him, waiting for the story of Geordie Sinclair's adventures, and he knew the unvarnished truth would not do. For his father's sake. Or for his own. Geordie's life, he saw clearly, had been based on fantasy. And it had been a failure.

So that story would not do.

He raised the empty tumbler meaningfully and waited till it was refilled. He took a swallow of the rough fiery liquid and began a carefully edited version of his father's life tailored to this audience.

'Yes, he got to the Klondike,' George began, 'and yes, he found gold.'

There was a rumble of excitement at that. He waited till it died down.

'He was one of the lucky ones. But when the Gold Rush ran out, he took himself down to San Francisco where he met my uncle Federico who brought him to Buenos Aires. There he met my mother...' George shrugged gracefully. 'And here I am.'

Questions were flung at him. George picked his way carefully through the minefield, giving away as little further information as possible.

'Ah yes,' he concluded. 'I am sorry. I should have said.' He spread his hands wide. 'My father died in Buenos Aires some thirty or more years ago. I was only a little boy.'

'Ah, that's a pity!' and the expressions of sympathy flowed. George sat back and listened to the memories of his father. Yes. He had been a petty criminal. A con-man. And definitely small-time.

'And yourself?' one of the men prodded. 'You were brought up over there?'

'You speak good English...' another added.

Ruby's eyes were on him, he noticed. He would need to choose his words with care. It was time to reinvent himself – to start out on a new path, the next stage of his own adventure – and he wanted it to go in his favour.

'I've spent some time in America,' George explained. 'My mother remarried – a cattle rancher and he had interests in the meat-packing business, for export. I... Shall we just say that school and my mother's new husband did not suit me...'

He waited for the understanding laughter to die down.

'I got sent to Chicago to learn the meat-packing business.' His eyes gleamed with amusement. 'But I found other things there of more interest to me.'

There was silence while his listeners took in what he was saying. Then, as he had hoped, the speculation began.

'Chicago?'

'That's where Al Capone...'

'Gangsters...'

'Bootlegging...'

George smiled. He nodded. 'That's right. I had a swell time!' He let the Chicago drawl colour his words. Ruby, he saw, was now watching him with wide-eyed admiration.

'Did you know that the great Al Capone only used Scots as his bodyguards? The hardest of the hard men?' George asked. His audience was clearly impressed.

'Of course it all came to an end when the Boss was arrested and even the Scots had to serve their time...' George raised his hands in mock surrender. 'Even me.'

That brought indrawn breath but again it was from folk who were impressed by his exploits.

George smiled. He had guessed his audience right.

'And then they deported us – to Glasgow! I have a Scottish name so that's why they sent me to Scotland. I thought, why not? I didn't want to go back to Argentina. So I've been in Glasgow for a while – with a few friends I made in Chicago. Then it got a little...' He glanced round the eager listeners. 'Shall I just say... uncomfortable!' He laughed, inviting them to join in. 'So I thought I'd come and take a look at Wick, see where my father was brought up. Maybe meet up with the family. See what opportunities there might be for a man like me...'

He leaned back and drained his whisky, his eyes fixed on Ruby. What happened now depended on her. Would she go along with that last statement? Or would she spill the beans about his humiliating search for his 'inheritance'? If she did, he would lose what credibility he had managed to create here.

Now that he knew there was no estate to inherit, no wealth, no castle, his options were few. He could not go back to Glasgow just yet. The police had got a little too close…

He was beginning to see possibilities – opportunities – here in Wick. He knew how to profit from a dry town where the prohibition of alcohol only made it a more attractive commodity. He had been part of Capone's operations for long enough. He could apply what he had learnt of the rackets there to his advantage here.

But to be held up to ridicule now, among these people, would destroy his chances of success before he ever got started. Among the criminal fraternity – even as small-scale as here – reputation mattered. If he was to set himself up in business, he would need the reputation of a hard man who knew what he was doing, not a romantic fool who ran after pipe dreams.

His eyes held Ruby's, daring her, challenging her to speak.

He waited. His future depended on her.

CHAPTER 9

It was chilly outside, with a stiff breeze off the sea.

Ruby waited till the door to the shebeen had shut firmly behind them before she asked, 'Now what?'

George looked into her eyes. He wanted to kiss her, but now was not the time and here was not the place. But he owed her. To his enormous relief Ruby had not blown his credibility. She had simply said 'Time we were going' and led the way out into the street.

'Back to town,' George said now, and she simply nodded and set off. He liked that. The girl knew how to fight her corner and she knew when to keep quiet.

They walked back to the centre of town in companionable silence and now stood once more outside the solicitor's office.

George gestured to his hotel. 'You could join me for dinner and I could express my gratitude...'

Ruby frowned. 'I don't think so,' she said. She held up her left hand with the tiny diamond sparkling on her engagement ring. 'It wouldn't do. People would see me, and talk.'

'And you're worried about that?' George challenged her. 'After where we've been?'

Ruby waved his question away.

'Oh, that doesn't matter. The place belongs to my uncle so nobody's surprised if I pop in from time to time. Sometimes I bring him in eggs from my mum in the country. Nobody thinks anything of that.'

'And me?' George asked silkily. 'What about going in there with me? Surely that's a bit different?'

Ruby shrugged and gave a quick grin. 'Well, you did come to the office the other day... so maybe I was just showing a passing tourist a bit of the town's low-life.'

'How kind.' There was ice underlying his words. He had begun to think perhaps he could become something more than a passing tourist.

Ruby brushed his displeasure away.

'So what are you going to do now? Will you stay at the hotel?' she asked, adding 'Can you stay at the hotel? Do you have enough money?'

George was startled into laughter. 'You're blunt, aren't you?'

With effort, he suppressed the sudden spasm of unease. Because yes, there was a problem. He had invested all his remaining funds in this trip to the land of his father in expectation of a significant return – that fantasy inheritance of castle and land and a new life as a local grandee. Now he would have to rebuild his stash.

Ruby read his silence correctly.

'I see. So what will you do? Have you got enough money to go back to Buenos Aires?'

George bridled, anger darkening his face. He would never, never go back there! How could he? Disowned for dishonouring the family name, they would never take him back. And he would never give them the chance.

'Right,' Ruby said, reading the answer in his face. 'And not Glasgow either?'

George thought of his hurried exit from that city. He had survived amongst the criminal fraternity there for a few years, but the police crackdown had made it uncomfortably hot for him to stay. And it was a miserable place, George thought, compared with Buenos Aires and Chicago. The slum tenements packed with the poor and hopeless... No, there was nothing for him there either.

'Mmm...' she said thoughtfully. 'So unless you've got somewhere else in mind, you're stuck here.'

George raised an eyebrow.

'And it looks like you won't be able to afford the hotel much longer.'

He gave her an abrupt nod. His mind was already racing. Somehow he had to get a toe-hold in this town so he could start the kind of liquor-running business he had in mind.

'Sounds as though you're going to need some kind of work,' Ruby said.

George snorted. Work? That was the last thing he wanted. Money. Now that was another thing, but he did not even have enough left for a decent stake in a poker game once he had paid his hotel bill. And if he wanted to stay in this town any length of time, he had better do the respectable thing and pay it.

'So what can you do?' Ruby asked. 'That's legal?'

George glared at her. Most of his activities had been illegal. But her question touched a nerve and he answered fast without thinking. 'I can drive.'

'Excellent!' Ruby's eyes lit up. 'That will do nicely. And you're already in touch with the right people.'

'What are you talking about?' George growled.

But Ruby simply gave him a triumphant grin. 'Cormack's Car Hire Company – where you hired your car the other day,' she spelled it out for him. 'They could surely use another driver. You already know the boss's daughter. Given the right incentive, I'm sure she'd put in a good word for you.'

George stared at her as she blithely added. 'And if I'm not mistaken, here comes Joyce now.' She gave George a gentle shove. 'This is your chance. Go and be nice to her. All you have to do is persuade her to get her dad to give you a job. And that's you sorted.'

Sorted?

Maybe not sorted, George thought, but as he rapidly reviewed Ruby's plan, he had to admit it offered possibilities. It would certainly get him started. He looked down the street in the direction Ruby had indicated. The pretty dark-haired child from the car hire office was walking their way.

'Why?' George asked Ruby, suddenly suspicious. 'Why are you helping me?'

'I like you,' she told him with another disarming grin. 'And it's a bit of fun, at the Cormacks' expense. They're a bit churchy. Ultra-respectable.' She sniffed. 'I'm not really respectable myself and they rub it in a bit. They don't think I'm good enough for their precious Bobby. But I've got him' – again the flash of the engagement ring – 'and maybe with you around, I can get him to come up to scratch and put a wedding ring on my finger. Then I can be respectable too, a lady of leisure...' She gave George a sly conspiratorial glance. 'So a bit of competition might be just what he needs.'

'I see,' George said. 'In that case, I'll have to see what I can do.'

'You do that,' Ruby said and slipped from his side.

CHAPTER 10

Joyce Cormack hurried along the main street, mentally ticking off the list of things she had planned to do. She had done some shopping for her mother, and now there might be time… She came to a sudden stop as she realised she had nearly bumped into someone standing in her way on the pavement. Her eyes flew wide open with horror as she saw who it was that she had so nearly collided with, and she took a rapid step back.

'Mr St Clair!'

Joyce bit her lip in a vain attempt to stop herself from blushing as she realised she had nearly bumped into him. She could feel the horrid heat flood her cheeks. He would think she was a complete idiot.

George raised his hat.

'Miss Cormack. How are you?'

His words were polite but his voice seemed strangely lacking in life. Looking into his face, Joyce was surprised to see that the debonair Argentinian was looking care-worn. At once, she asked, 'More to the point, how are you? You don't look so happy today. Is there anything I can do to help?'

George waved a hand in the direction of the solicitor's office. 'I don't think anyone can help,' he said with a sad shrug.

'Oh, I'm sorry,' Joyce said, thinking quickly. 'The family business you were seeing to. Not good news?

George nodded. 'Not good. But there it is and nothing can be done about it.' He made to move away.

Joyce hesitated only for a moment.

'Would it help to talk about it? Maybe over a cup of tea?' She paused and added, trying to sound grown-up and sophisticated, 'Unless you'd prefer a drink? That would be more difficult. The town's dry... but I'm sure your hotel...' She ground doubtfully to a halt.

'No. Tea will do nicely,' George said. 'I'm not much of a one for drink.'

'Oh, that's good,' Joyce said with a relieved smile. She did not know what she would have done if he had wanted a drink. She had never been to a bar in her life and her father would probably disown her if she did go into one. 'My family don't drink either. This way then,' and she led him away from the solicitor's office and across the bridge that joined the two halves of the town. They walked up a steep road and entered a cosy tearoom.

Settled at a table in the warmth of the tearoom, Joyce ordered tea and scones for them both. As they waited for the food to arrive, she smiled reassuringly at him and began to try to draw him out.

'I hope it isn't really so bad,' she said sympathetically. Her mother had often told her she was making mountains out of molehills of little worries and she hoped that would be the case in this instance.

But George ran a hand through his thick black hair, his face deeply worried. 'Oh, I'm afraid it is.'

Joyce raised an eyebrow, encouraging him to continue.

'I had hopes,' he explained with rueful simplicity. 'Such hopes. But it seems that's all they were...'

They were interrupted by the arrival of a waitress with a pot of tea and a plate of liberally buttered scones. Joyce thanked the girl and set about pouring the tea, checking whether George took his tea with milk and sugar. As she handed him his cup and offered him the plate of scones, she asked, 'Would you like to tell me about it?'

George took a ragged breath and said, 'It can't do any more harm.' He sighed again. 'My father came from here. From Wick. And he told my mother he was a rich man, with land, even a castle.' He shrugged. 'He died when I was small so all I had of him were my mother's stories. All my life I dreamed of coming here and claiming my inheritance.'

Joyce nodded her understanding, her clear brown eyes fixed on his face.

George continued, 'At last I managed to get here.' He waved a hand. 'It's a long story but not important. What is important is that I used every penny I had to get here only to discover...' He paused, swallowing hard.

'Yes?' Joyce prompted, though she feared she knew what was coming.

'Only to discover that my father had not been telling my mother the truth.' George's mouth turned down in disappointment and he shrugged again, that continental gesture that so fascinated Joyce. 'There is no land, no castle, no money,' he said. 'And I am here, far from home. My hopes in ruins and me, looking and feeling like a fool. I am only glad my mother is not here to see it.'

Joyce's heart went out to him. She saw the truth in his eyes, saw the terrible destruction of his hopes. But even at this moment of deep disappointment, his first thought was for his widowed mother who had been so deceived. She reached across the table and patted his hand.

'Don't worry,' she told him. 'You're not the first and you won't be the last.'

'What do you mean?' George asked.

'So many people left this county over the years for a better life somewhere else,' Joyce explained. 'And plenty of them spun tall stories about their life back home. Then their descendants turn up hoping for castles and land and money... It's not uncommon.' She smiled gently.

George seemed to brace himself.

'Well, that is my story,' he said. 'I suppose I'm glad it's not uncommon. But now I am in a fix. My money will run out soon. And I have no idea what I'm going to do.' He added intently, 'But somehow I must find a way to get home. There must be a way...' He looked into Joyce's sympathetic eyes. 'I'm willing to do anything to pay my way – not that I'm trained for much! My stepfather had a cattle ranch and was involved in the meat-packing business. I learned that from him. But I don't see much need for that round here!'

'No,' Joyce agreed, her mind working furiously. 'This isn't cattle country. Is there anything else you can do?'

'I can drive.' George shrugged again, dismissively.

Joyce gazed at him over the rim of her cup, her brown eyes kind and thoughtful.

'Mmm,' she pondered. 'I wonder. Would you be willing to drive as a job? I know it's not what you're used to – but just for a while, just till you get yourself sorted out, decide what you want to do?'

'Drive?' George queried. He stared at her blankly, then as if suddenly understanding, asked, 'Like your brother Bobby did for me? Taking people out?'

'Yes, like that, if Dad could find you a job,' Joyce agreed. 'But other things too – the ambulance...' She hesitated, then asked, 'And the hearse... would you mind that?'

George smiled. 'A job is a job is a job,' he told her firmly. 'I would be grateful to do whatever I was asked.'

'In that case, I will need to talk to my father.' Joyce looked at her watch. 'Oh, is that the time? I must go.' She indicated the tea. 'I'll pay for this so don't even think of arguing! I'll talk to my dad and see what we can do.' As she gathered up her coat and handbag, she asked, 'You'll be staying at the hotel for a day or two?'

'I have nowhere else to go,' George said simply.

'Ah yes,' Joyce said. 'We'll have to think about that too. Don't worry,' she told him softly. 'As my mum always says, God's in charge so everything will work out all right.'

She headed for the counter to pay for their tea, then with a grin and a wave, was gone.

CHAPTER 11

'And he can drive?' Rab Cormack queried.

'Oh yes,' Joyce told her father confidently. She had raised the subject while the family were having their evening meal and was delighted when her brother Bobby stepped in to back her up.

'Aye, that's right,' Bobby said. 'He said so when we were out the other day. He learned in Argentina and he did a lot of driving when he was in Chicago.'

'But his prospects have turned out to be not so bright?' Danny enquired drily.

'Like so many before him,' their mother said. She smiled at her husband. 'So many young folk are in a hurry to get away and make their fortune that maybe would have done better to stay home.'

In their youth she and Rab had been the ones in their circle to stay at home while others had set off on great adventures.

'We didn't do so badly,' he acknowledged. He smiled at his daughter. 'I'll give the lad a chance. It's our Christian duty to help those who have fallen on hard times and it seems he's willing to work to help himself out of it. Tell him to come and see me and we'll give him a test drive. See how he does.'

And so it was that George St Clair presented himself once more at the sliding window in the office of the Cormack Car Hire Company. Ruby and Joyce exchanged glances and rose as one.

'Mr St Clair!'

George bowed. 'Ladies.'

'I'll get Dad,' Joyce said and hurried out of the office.

'Well done,' Ruby said with a conspiratorial grin. 'So far, so good.'

George returned the grin. 'I owe you a drink.'

'And if you get the job?' she teased cheekily.

'I'll owe you more than a drink,' he told her, his dark eyes glinting, 'and I'll have the money to pay for it!'

'I'll hold you to that,' Ruby told him.

'In my country, it's the men who do the holding...' George said.

Ruby grinned. 'Is that so?'

George smiled. 'You'll see. If I get the job...' He stopped and corrected himself. '*When* I get the job...'

The outside door opened and Ruby returned rapidly to her desk, her colour bright. George turned to see a slightly stooped older man enter, followed by Joyce.

'Dad, this is Mr St Clair,' she said, and went back to her desk in the inner office, leaving them alone.

The older man looked George up and down, his eyes betraying nothing of what he was thinking.

'So you're interested in a job with us?' the man asked bluntly.

'Yes, *señor*. I... I need a job,' George said. He felt rather than saw Ruby's amusement at his humble tones before she busied herself at her desk.

'Is that so?' The older man pierced him with a quizzical gaze. 'Come through to the house, Mr St Clair, and we'll have a wee word.'

He gestured to the door into the inner office and then the door through to the house.

George went through and the older man followed him into a comfortably furnished sitting room, taking up his stance by a fireplace where a cheerful fire was burning in the grate.

He looked at George, assessingly.

'I can use another driver,' he said. 'There's a war coming and my lads are itching to join up. I'll need able-bodied men in the garage and Joyce tells me you can drive. Is that right?'

'Yes,' George replied. 'Since I was young. My country has many cars. America too. It is the accepted thing.'

Rab Cormack nodded.

'But we drive on the other side of the road...' George paused. 'Though I did a bit of driving in Glasgow,' he added.

'I see.' The older man considered. 'You might need a bit of practice. Have you only driven for your own pleasure? Can you take orders, look after passengers...?'

George thought back to the innumerable times he had driven Al Capone's wife Mary to the hairdresser's. That definitely counted as dealing with passengers. And the bootlegging, bringing in illicit bourbon and whiskey to the customers, and ensuring the Boss got paid – that would count as taking orders. He suppressed a grin. So long as he was not asked for the details, he should pass on both counts.

'Yes, *señor*,' he replied, schooling his face to seriousness. 'I have experience of both.'

Rab nodded. 'Good. We do a variety of types of hires,' he continued, and proceeded to describe the business – a general taxi service for shorter and longer trips, weddings, funerals, and so on.

George managed to maintain an expression of polite interest but his patience was fraying. Honest employment and a boring honest employer like this tedious old man were uncharted territory. He comforted himself with the thought that the pert blonde in the office might provide a little much-needed entertainment if he was going to stick around long enough to recoup his losses.

He suddenly realised he had been asked a question. Hastily he tried to recall what the older man had been saying.

'Why do you need the job?'

George's brain snapped to attention. He would need to be careful. Which version of his story would work best here?

'My father died when I was very young,' he began. 'My mother, who had led a rather sheltered, protected life in Argentina, believed him to be a man of some standing and wealth in his homeland. Here. Caithness.'

George watched the older man following his story. He continued, 'Back in Buenos Aires my mother remarried and now has many children with my stepfather. Though he was kind to me, it is only right that it is his sons who inherit his business – so I came to discover my father's estate.' George spread his hands wide. 'I saved up and have spent every penny to come. Only to discover that my father...'

He paused. 'Only to discover when I went to see the solicitor that my father had exaggerated somewhat.' He gave a rueful smile.

Rab's eyes narrowed as he considered George's words.

'I see,' Rab said. 'You mean...?'

'I mean there was nothing to inherit.' The words came out harshly.

'I see. Nothing to inherit? No estate. So...'

'So I have very little money left. I need a job – so I can earn my keep, and save enough to cover my passage back home.'

'I see,' Rab said again. He fixed George with his eyes. 'Well, it'll do no harm to give you a try. See what you can do. Come through to

49

the garage with me and you can take one of the cars out. I'll be the passenger.' He looked sharply at George. 'You can read a map?'

'Yes, *señor*,' George said.

'You'll need to learn the roads and places before you'll be able to drive on your own,' Rab cautioned.

'I learn fast,' George assured him. He thought back to the maze of streets that was Chicago, the warren that was Glasgow. This little backwater would be no problem.

'And we can't call you Mr St Clair,' Rab said. 'What's your Christian name?'

'I was baptised Jorge.' He pronounced it the Spanish way, *Horrhay*. Seeing with amusement Rab Cormack's recoil, he added, 'That's the Spanish for George.'

Relief eased Rab's features. 'Well, I don't think folks round here will manage the Spanish very well,' he said. 'How would you feel about being George?'

'*Señor*, it's all the same to me. I'm happy to be George.' In his thoughts, George sent a toast to his father. From one George to another.

'Then George you will be,' Rab Cormack said as he led the way to a gleaming black Rover that sat at the kerb waiting to be taken out. He waved a proudly proprietorial arm at it.

'In you get, George. Let's see what you can do.'

CHAPTER 12

Joyce's eyes sparkled.

'Thank you, Daddy!' she said and she leaned over to plant a kiss on his cheek.

Rab Cormack waved the affectionate expression of gratitude away.

'We could do with another driver,' he said. 'And anyway, he's only on probation. If he can't learn the roads or doesn't get on with the passengers, he won't be staying.'

'He'll be fine,' Bobby said. 'He's been driving for years.'

'I'm sure he'll manage,' Joyce agreed, but a little anxiously. The small grey town of Wick with its sharp corners and steep braes was a lot different from what George St Clair was surely used to in the big cities. And the country roads with their hump-back bridges and occasional straying sheep offered different challenges.

'We'll try him out on a few local hires to start with, just around the town, till he gets the hang of the cars and the roads,' Joyce's father instructed her. 'Don't book him for anything else till I tell you.'

Joyce nodded happily. She was sure George was going to be a great asset to the firm.

'And the ladies will love him,' Danny put in with a satirical grin. 'Like our Joyce, they'll all fall for his continental charm. You'll have to fight them off if you're going to stand a chance, sister mine!'

'Don't be horrid!' Joyce told her brother.

But as the days and weeks progressed and George settled into his new job with the firm, she had to admit to a frisson of jealousy. It was soon clear that he was very much in demand as the chauffeur of choice among the well-off older ladies of the town. There was a certain cachet in being driven around by such an exotic, handsome and helpful chauffeur.

Even Ruby seemed to brighten up when George was around. Gone was the bored and sulky girl she used to be, forever moaning discontentedly about everything. Instead she was lively and... could it be, flirtatious? Joyce frowned as she thought about Ruby's behaviour. She reminded herself sternly that Ruby loved Bobby – didn't she? It was only because Bobby would not name the day for their wedding that she had been complaining so much. Yes, of course, Ruby loved Bobby. George de la Vega St Clair – how Joyce loved to roll his name round in her mind – George was simply a charming and attractive man and Ruby was merely having a little naughty but completely innocent fun, playing games, trying to make Bobby jealous.

It would not work, Joyce thought. She could have told Ruby that. Bobby was hopelessly in love with Ruby and would never think a disloyal or critical thought about her. He had made his choice and stuck to it even in the face of his parents' disapproval. Nothing and nobody could ever separate him from Ruby. In any case, he and George had become inseparable friends since George had begun driving for their father. In fact, George had become very much a fixture both in the business and in their family as Bobby had got in the habit of bringing him home and including him in family occasions.

'He's on his own and far from home,' Bobby had explained. 'It's the least we can do, the Christian thing to do, to be friendly to him.'

And so to Joyce's delight, George fitted perfectly into their lives. Though she soon discovered that simply seeing him at work and with Bobby was not enough for her. She longed to have time alone with George, to get to know him better. She often recalled with delight that brief time they had spent together at the tearoom when he had opened his heart to her.

But how could she create another opportunity like that? Without looking... Here she took herself firmly to task. Without looking exactly what she was. Interested in him.

CHAPTER 13

'No,' Rab Cormack said.

'But, Dad...!' Joyce protested. '*Everybody* will be going! Why can't I?'

'Joyce,' her mother said warningly. 'Finish your breakfast.'

Joyce sighed. She knew her father's word was law, but she had hoped that just this once she would be able to make him change his mind. She so wanted to go...

Everybody would be going to that evening's dance out at Ackergill. George would be sure to be there. And if *he* were there and *she* were there, then surely – even just out of politeness – he would have to dance with her... at least once? She bit her lip in frustration. This was surely the opportunity she had been waiting for.

But she knew her father did not really approve of young girls going to these country dances. And there was no way he would permit her to go on her own. He was occasionally willing to sanction her going to a carefully selected dance with her cousin Anne. Anne was reliable, responsible, a few years older than Joyce and happy to provide both company and token chaperonage. But Anne was away and there was no one else that her father would approve of to accompany her.

So she could not go.

Joyce tried to force down her rebellion with her breakfast, but once at her desk in the office, it had forced its way back into the front of her mind. Why couldn't she go to the dance? It just wasn't fair!

'Why are you so sad today, *chiquita*?'

Joyce jumped. She had been so lost in her thoughts that George and her brother Bobby had come into the office unnoticed. Swiftly she smiled at George. She caught her brother's mocking gaze and looked away, shuffling some invoices on her desk and trying to ignore him. But of course where George was, Bobby would be.

They could not be more different, she thought. George in his dark blue suit, holding his driver's cap in his hand, looked very much the part of a very high-class chauffeur. Beside him her older brother was as usual decked out in oil-stained overalls. Bobby much preferred tinkering with the vehicles in his care rather than driving folk around in them, as the oil stains on his overalls and his hands attested.

'Come now,' George coaxed her. 'It can't be so bad?'

Joyce roused herself from her misery to smile at him and shake her head.

'Will you tell me what it's about?' he pressed. 'Maybe I can help?'

'Joyce.'

It was her father's voice. She guiltily broke eye contact with George. She had not noticed her father's arrival either. Oh dear, this daydreaming and mooning over George just would not do!

'My dear, is there some problem that I don't know about?' Her father sounded confused.

As embarrassment flooded a rush of hot blood into her cheeks, sudden anger at this betrayal of her feelings made her blurt out, 'But you know all about it, Daddy! The only problem is that you've said no!'

Her father stared at her.

'Did I? What about?'

'Tonight's dance – at Ackergill,' Joyce reminded him. 'You said I couldn't go...'

'Oh that,' her father said. 'I thought we'd dealt with that. You know it's different when your cousin Anne is here and you can go with her, but she's away, so you'd be on your own... I'm sorry but it's still no. Your mother and I could not allow it.' He smiled, trying to lighten the refusal. 'Come now. Anne will be home soon and there will be plenty more dances...'

Joyce's mouth tightened in frustration. She wanted to go to *this* dance! George might go away soon, despite what he said, and then there would never be another chance...

That he was still here was a bonus. They had not expected him to stay so long, but as the weeks progressed, George insisted that he was happy doing what he was doing. Maybe he would stay a bit longer... Maybe there was no rush to return to Buenos Aires.

'And Caithness,' he had declared, 'it begins to feel like home.'

Joyce now glanced up at George, her frustration at her father's refusal clear in her eyes. George winked at her with a quick smile, then turned to her father.

'But if there were a party of, say three or four young people, friends of the family, for Joyce to go with... that would be different, no?'

'As you say,' Rab Cormack acquiesced. 'That would be different.'

'I think,' George said, 'that if Miss Joyce will check the book, she will find that there is a hire to that dance tonight and there would be room for her to join the party.' He gave that funny little bow. 'And if it would put your mind at rest, I will be happy to drive the party to the dance myself, and make sure that Miss Joyce gets home safely at whatever time you deem appropriate.'

Rab shifted his weight from one foot to another as he pondered. Joyce hid her excitement. George had neatly outmanoeuvred her father.

'Say yes, Daddy! Please say yes!'

Joyce waited for his reply, her eyes shining with delight.

Rab frowned.

'Do we know who the people in this party are?' he parried. 'You say "friends of the family"?'

'Yes, of course,' George said with a smile. 'It includes your own son!' Bobby started in surprise but George threw him a meaningful glance. After a moment's hesitation, Bobby grinned and nodded.

'That's right,' Bobby said. 'Me and Ruby will be there. She'll be perfectly safe with us.'

'In that case,' Rab said slowly, 'I think it will be all right for Joyce to go with you. But she must be home by midnight.'

Joyce threw George a sparkling glance and beamed at her father.

'Thank you, Daddy!'

CHAPTER 14

Joyce settled back to her work, smiling blissfully. George had come to her rescue! Oh, surely that meant he would dance with her tonight? It would be wonderful. She could just imagine… But what was she going to wear?

As the thoughts raced across her mind, she barely heard her brother saying, 'What was that about? I wasn't planning on taking Ruby to the dance at Ackergill tonight!'

George reached for the hire book and began to write in it. Blotting the ink carefully, he replaced it on Joyce's desk, smiled at her, then took Bobby's arm to lead him away.

'So what were you planning to do? I'm sure your fiancée would enjoy a night of dancing,' George said. 'And it would be fun – the four of us out for an evening together.'

Bobby grinned. 'That's true. I haven't taken Ruby to a dance out of town for ages.' He slapped George on the back. 'That's a great idea!'

And when the big black car arrived at the family home later that evening, Bobby was as enthusiastic about the outing as Joyce.

'You're both looking very fine,' their mother said as she waved them goodbye. Bobby shuffled sheepishly but Joyce glowed. A new dress and a smart hairstyle had, she felt, worked wonders and as she allowed George to help her into the car, she accepted his appreciative glances as her due.

Ruby was already seated in the car. Her dress was clearly the very latest fashion and, beside her, Joyce felt suddenly very young and rather dowdy. Bobby planted himself cheerfully in the middle of the big back seat with the girls on either side of him.

'I'm a lucky man!' he declared. 'I have a beauty on each side of me.'

Ruby laughed. 'Why, thank you, kind sir!' she declared. 'Come on, driver, what are we waiting for? The night is young and so are we! Let's go and have some fun before we're too much older!'

She laughed loudly at this and Bobby joined in the laughter. Joyce huddled down in the seat by the window. She hoped, once they arrived at the dance, that she and George could leave Bobby and Ruby behind. She really did not want to be stuck in a foursome with them all night. She wanted George to herself...

The thought pushed all others from her mind, and the rest of the journey was spent daydreaming.

~

'You're looking lovely tonight,' George murmured as he gave Joyce his arm and led her into the village hall where the dance was being held.

'Thank you,' Joyce whispered, barely able to believe her ears. She could feel herself glow with delight.

She caught sight of Bobby helping Ruby out of the car. He was so in love with her, Joyce thought. If only George could fall in love with her like that... Joyce marshalled her thoughts. Tonight was her first real chance to win George's heart. Bobby was concentrating on Ruby.

That would keep him occupied for the evening and out of her way. An interfering big brother, however benevolent, was not welcome! And the bold, rather brash Ruby was competition she did not need for George's attention – even if George's reactions to Ruby were only out of politeness.

In the hall, the band was already set up on the stage and the dance in full swing. The cheery toe-tapping music of the accordion and the fiddle filled the hall, competing with the happy chatter of the dancers. Cigarette smoke drifted up to the ceiling.

George watched the dancers as they twirled in a lively reel. His face was a picture of bemusement.

'What's the matter?' Joyce asked.

George waved a hand at the dance floor. 'I'm afraid I do not know how to do this kind of dance! We do not have this in Buenos Aires!'

'Well, you wouldn't,' Joyce replied. 'These are Scottish dances.' She paused, then added hopefully, 'If you like, I could teach you?'

Dark eyes smiled into hers. 'That would be most kind, but perhaps I should watch for a while and you could explain…'

He led Joyce to a quiet space where chairs had been set out. Joyce acquiesced, though sitting out the dance with George had not featured in her dreams. Hopefully there would be some dance on the evening's programme that he was able to do!

The evening progressed comfortably as Joyce explained how the various Scottish dances were performed. George brought refreshments, and otherwise remained, to her delight, by her side. Although other would-be partners approached from time to time, George's proprietorial glower seemed to put them off and Joyce was happy to offer them a smile but remain with George.

Then as the evening drew to a close, the band struck up a waltz. George rose and offered his hand.

'Now this,' he said, 'is a dance I do know how to dance!'

Her breath catching with excitement, Joyce took his hand and allowed him to guide her onto the floor. As he gathered her into his arms, she caught a glimpse of Ruby dancing with her brother. For a moment she thought she saw a flash of something in Ruby's eyes, something she could not quite make out, but the next moment the music had whirled them away and she was caught up in her first dance with George, aware only of his arms around her, his overwhelming closeness.

So this was love, Joyce thought, and blissfully closed her eyes.

CHAPTER 15

The stars in Joyce's eyes rivalled those in the velvet night sky when George brought her home at the appointed hour. Bobby and Ruby had arranged to return later with a friend and neither George nor Joyce had protested.

George opened the car door for Joyce with a flourish and handed her out. As she paused at the door of her home, he bowed with sudden graceful ceremony and placed a kiss on her fingertips.

'Good night, *chiquita*,' he murmured. 'Sleep well.'

Her dazzled eyes watched him climb back into the big black car and drive away, then almost sleepwalking, she let herself into the house. Hanging up her coat in the hallway, she drifted as if on air up the stairs to her room. But as she passed her parents' bedroom, she heard her mother call out, 'Is that you, darling?'

'Yes, Mum.' Joyce pushed the door open a crack and popped her head in. 'I had a lovely evening!'

'That's good, dear. You can tell me all about it in the morning. Time for bed now!'

'Yes, Mum. Good night.'

As the door closed she heard the rumble of her father's deep voice, but she was so happy she hurried to her room, her mind filled with the joys of her evening with George.

'He's too old for her,' her father muttered.

'Sometimes that's no bad thing,' her mother countered gently.

'She's too young,' he persisted.

'Not so very young,' Hannah said. 'And if George is serious, surely he'll be wise enough to take his time courting her.'

Her husband shook his head doubtfully. 'There's just something about the fellow.'

'Oh Rab,' Hannah protested. 'Is it just because he's foreign? He's turned out to be a good worker, hasn't he, and he's brought a lot of business in?'

Rab snorted. 'Not so surprising, is it? There's no fool like an old fool and there's plenty of those in Wick – all those wealthy older ladies looking for a bit of excitement. He's got himself quite a fan club.'

'But he hasn't put a foot wrong, has he?' Hannah asked.

Again, Rab shook his head. 'No. I'll give him that. He seems able to keep his nose clean.'

'And you'd hear, wouldn't you?'

'Oh yes, I'd soon hear about it.'

'So what's the problem?'

Rab sighed. 'I don't know. I just can't completely take to the fellow. There just seems to be something...'

'Bobby likes him,' Hannah offered. 'They've become good friends – and I'm glad. It's good for Bobby to have friends his own age.'

'It's time Bobby was settling down,' his father said.

'Well, if that's the case, then the same thing applies to George. There's little difference in their age, is there?'

'About a year.'

'Well then.'

'Women!' Rab said affectionately as he turned on his side and got comfortable. 'Always have to have the last word.'

Hannah smiled and snuggled down beside him. But she had to admit to her own niggle of unease about George St Clair. There was, as her husband said, just something about the fellow. Was it that somehow he seemed just a little too good to be true?

CHAPTER 16

Back in his digs, George lounged comfortably in an armchair beside the fire. On the table beside him, a cigarette smouldered in an ashtray and a tumbler with a couple of fingers of bootlegged whisky sat alongside.

Footsteps hurried up the stairs, then the door was flung open and Ruby stood there, her face aflame with anger.

'Just what do you think you're playing at?' she demanded. 'It was your stupid idea, this outing to Ackergill, wasn't it? All four of us, together!'

She slammed the door shut and marched into the room.

'Do you really think Bobby is stupid?' she threw at George. 'After all the trouble I've taken to pull the wool over his eyes! If you're not careful, one of these days he'll find out about us!' She glared at him. 'And Joyce may be eighteen but she's still just a kid! She's a complete innocent. You shouldn't mess around with her!'

George reached for his glass and took a slow sip of the whisky. 'Anyone would think you care about them,' he said softly.

Ruby took a threatening step towards him. He watched with an appreciative smile playing on his mouth. Her anger always made her more attractive to him.

'Well?' she said, standing in front of him, arms akimbo. 'You've got some explaining to do!'

George's eyes narrowed. 'So just exactly what is your problem?' he asked quietly.

'Are you going to leave her alone?' Ruby demanded.

'Why should I?' George taunted. 'Because she's an innocent and not safe with the likes of me? Or because you're jealous?'

He took a second unhurried sip of his whisky and then waved the tumbler at the bottle.

'Get yourself a drink and come and sit down. You really mustn't worry. You have nothing to worry about.'

Ruby threw him a mutinous glare.

'Calm down and let me explain!' George said, and picked up his cigarette.

The look Ruby threw at him sizzled with fury, but he ignored it and waited till she had splashed some whisky into a second tumbler and taken it to the chair on the other side of the hearth from his.

'This had better be good,' she said, flinging herself gracelessly into the chair.

'Oh, it will be,' George assured her. He took a leisurely draw at his cigarette then stubbed it out in the ashtray. 'Now,' he said. 'You and I like the nice things of life, yes?'

'Yes,' she agreed, slowly sipping the whisky.

'And those things cost money?'

She nodded, more impatiently.

'And we currently don't have enough money for the things we'd really like, despite our jobs and the little things we find to do outside of work?'

Ruby raised an eyebrow. She had been instrumental in introducing George to the right kind of people to make the enterprise a success. Not only that, but she organised which hires he could utilise. He drove and managed the cargoes. And they shared the income from the hidden cargoes of outlawed alcohol that George brought back to customers in Wick from hires to the country areas where there was no prohibition.

But George was right. The money they had made up till now did not go far. She frowned.

'So,' George said. 'I've thought of a nice, easy way to make sure we get the life we want.' He sat back, satisfaction on his face.

'Nice, easy' sounded good but Ruby's eyes narrowed suspiciously. There had to be a catch.

'So what's your bright idea?' Ruby asked. 'Exactly what do you have in mind?'

'The Cormacks,' George announced with a flourish, like a conjurer pulling a rabbit from a hat. 'And their business. They're like ripe fruit waiting to be plucked – so innocent and unsuspecting – and here are you and me, ready and able to do the plucking.'

'Just what are you talking about?' Ruby demanded. 'I've already got Bobby on a string, and when we're married...'

'Ah yes,' George said. 'When you're married, then you'll be a lady of leisure. And later on, dear Bobby will inherit the business from his father, and that nice house you've been admiring. All of that is yours for the taking.'

Ruby glared at him. 'I know all that,' she said scornfully. 'That's why I've invested so much time and trouble on him – and I don't want it messed up now!'

George nodded. 'Agreed. It's important that you go on with your plan. You marry Bobby.'

Ruby nodded, warily.

'And I won't be so far away,' George said. 'What's going to happen is that I'll marry the sister. Tonight was just the beginning of our happy foursome...' He sat back with a pleased smile on his face.

'You're never serious?' Ruby stared at him.

'I am,' George replied. 'It's obvious she's interested – and willing.'

'They'd never allow it,' Ruby breathed. 'I had a tough enough time with Bobby, but Joyce...'

'They will if they have to,' George said confidently.

Ruby's eyes widened. 'You wouldn't?'

'Wouldn't I?' George said dismissively. 'This is the plan. Between the pair of us, we get our hands firmly on the business – which provides us with access to the cars we need, a secure legal income, and the assured continuation of our other interests without any fear of interference.'

'But Mr Cormack – and Bobby?' Ruby said. 'What about them?'

'They need never know,' George said. 'You can play your part, can't you? For as long as it's required? They'll have no need to question anything, till it's too late.'

Ruby nodded, but she chewed her lip as she thought over the implications of George's words.

'It won't be for ever,' George assured her. 'Just till we have everything sewn up. As son-in-law, I'm sure I'll soon be made a partner in the business and then between us we can milk it.'

'But what about you and me?' Ruby asked. 'I thought...' She took a deep breath. 'George...'

'You thought right,' George said. 'We'll just have to be a little more careful for a while, that's all, but there's no reason why you-and-me should not continue...'

He rose and refreshed his drink, giving Ruby time to digest the plan.

'So what do you say?' he asked. 'Are you in it for the long haul? You marry Bobby, I marry Joyce. We get our hands on the business and the money...'

Ruby hesitated for a moment. 'Yes, I can see it would work,' she said thoughtfully.

'So? Are you in?'

Ruby raised her eyes to his, dark calculating eyes meeting dark calculating eyes. Slowly she smiled.

'Why not? I'm in,' she said.

George raised his glass in a toast.

'To us, and a whole better future!'

Ruby copied him with a grin.

As she swallowed the whisky, George said with a smile, 'Tonight was a good start. Maybe we should be planning for a double wedding?'

Ruby exploded into laughter. 'Oh, that would be funny!'

George dropped a kiss on her head and offered her his hand.

'Bed?' he asked.

CHAPTER 17

Manitoba, Canada, 1938

Steeling himself, Hugh Mackay stepped inside the familiar little Presbyterian church and made his way to his mother's side.

'Hugh!'

The pretty older woman accepted his kiss of greeting with a smile. But her brow furrowed as she strained to look past his broad frame down the aisle to the door.

'But where are Katie and little Hugo?' She frowned. 'They're not with you today? Are they all right?'

Hugh's face tightened. He knew he would have to tell her. He desperately needed her help. That was why he had come. His worries churned and choked him. But where to begin? Gratefully he realised the congregation was standing up as the Bible was brought into church followed by the minister in his black robes. The service was about to start.

'Later,' Hugh muttered with relief. 'I'll tell you later.'

Maybe by the end of the service, he would be able to voice his worries. Maybe the service would help.

But an hour later as he followed his mother out of the little church where her beloved Clem had pastored for so many years, Hugh's heart was as heavy as when he had set out from home. He schooled himself to shake hands politely with the new minister and bat away the kind enquiries of the friends who lingered outside.

'Come,' Hugh said. 'I'll take you home and then we can talk.'

Nancy raised an eyebrow. 'Since when did one of my menfolk offer to talk?' she asked with a teasing smile. But there was no answering grin from Hugh. His face was set and grim.

At the little house in town where Nancy had settled after Clem died, Hugh helped her down from the buggy. She opened the door and preceded him into the hallway.

'Coffee?' she asked, leading the way into the kitchen. Without waiting for a reply, she poured a mugful from the ever-hot coffee pot on the top of the range, added cream and sugar and handed it to him. She pointed to one of the chairs by the table, and Hugh with a wry smile obediently sat down.

So many times over the years they had gone through this routine. Hugh set down the mug and stroked the smooth worn surface of the table. It was a solid old table, familiar and comforting. Whenever he had had a worry or a problem – or had got into trouble of any kind – his mother would bring him into the comforting warmth of her kitchen with its delicious cooking or baking smells and get whatever it was sorted out.

Hugh smiled. It had been a good upbringing and he was grateful for it. His mother had been through a lot for him. A young girl, pregnant and alone in the wilds of Canada, yet she had managed to survive. After his father, Hughie Mackay, was killed, she had made her way to Hughie's relatives in Manitoba. Bill and Marie had taken her in and looked after her – and him when he made his appearance.

Through Bill and Marie, Nancy had met Pastor Clem. They had fallen in love and shared many years of happiness together till Clem died. Hugh thought of Clem fondly. He had been a good man and a wise one. Though Hugh had lived with his mother and Clem in town where Clem had his pastorate, he had been allowed to spend as much time as he liked out at the ranch with Bill and Marie.

How glad Hugh was that his mother had made her way to the Alexander ranch. He had inherited it and now ran it. Hugh's thoughts faltered as he thought of the home he had left that morning.

They had been so happy! When he had married his darling Katie, he had not thought it possible to be any happier! But then Hugo had arrived – the apple of his eye, his pride and joy. All the clichés and all true.

He loved his little family. He loved the ranch. He loved the home he had made for them, the life they shared together.

Hugh pulled the mug of coffee towards him and downed a long swallow. Where had he gone wrong? How could it all have gone so wrong?

CHAPTER 18

'Tell me,' Nancy said quietly as she settled down opposite him at the old wooden table, a mug of coffee wrapped between her hands. Her loving eyes focused steadily on her son's face. 'You know I'll do anything I can to help. I love you, son, and I love Katie and Hugo.'

To Hugh's horror, tears pricked at his eyes. He set his mug of coffee down shakily and scrubbed the tears out of the way.

'Darling, what's the matter?' His mother's voice was filled with kindly concern. 'Is it really so bad?'

'Oh Mum,' Hugh groaned. 'I'm so worried...'

She reached across and squeezed his arm.

'Get it all out,' she said. 'That's the best thing.'

Hugh managed a sickly grin. It was what she always said, no matter what the problem was. But this time...

He took a deep breath and plunged in. It could not wait any longer.

'It's Katie. She's ill. And she's in pain, I'm sure of it.' He shook his head, trying to clear his thoughts. 'She's not managing to hide it any longer. She's not up to looking after Hugo any more, or the house... She's got no energy, no interest, but she insists on trying and...'

He could hear the raw pain in his voice. He struggled to go on, to tell his mother exactly how it was.

'She won't listen to me that she needs help. And she won't go to the doctor.' Hugh's voice wobbled as he confessed the unthinkable. 'We've even had words about it.'

He put his head in his hands. He had said it now. The unthinkable. Their happy marriage was in tatters. It was out in the open. There was nothing more he could do.

'What about her parents? Katie's mum?' Nancy probed. 'Does she know?'

Hugh shook his head. 'Since they moved to Calgary, we haven't seen much of them for a while. And Katie insists she's not that ill and they don't need to be bothered. But she is!'

His voice broke alarmingly as he said it.

'Should you write to Katie's mum and tell her?' Nancy suggested.

Hugh's shoulders slumped in defeat. 'She'd never forgive me.' Losing the Katie he loved was bad enough without losing her love for him along the way.

'But what about telling me? Won't she be cross about that?'

'I don't know! I don't know what to do any more!' Desperation welled up inside him. 'But I've got to do something! The only thing I could think of was to come to you. I thought you'd have some idea what to do.'

'Yes, my love,' Nancy said soothingly. 'And you've done the right thing. I do think we should tell Katie's mum and dad, but first I think I need to come out to the ranch and take a look at her for myself. See what's going on. See just how bad this is.'

Hugh felt a sudden surge of hope. Maybe his mother would see what the problem was. He knew it was some woman's thing Katie would not talk to him about. She would be able to help Katie get it fixed. Maybe things were not as bad as he feared?

74

He felt his shoulders relax.

'That would be good,' he said. 'Maybe leave it for a few days so she doesn't connect your arrival with my trip to town?'

Nancy nodded. 'I haven't seen young Hugo for a little while so maybe it's time his grandma came out to the ranch for a visit?'

CHAPTER 19

'Oh, Nancy! I didn't know you were coming! Were we expecting you and I forgot? I'm so sorry… The house isn't prepared for visitors…'

'I'm not a visitor, my love,' Nancy began, fearing Katie would burst into tears, but welcome distraction came with running footsteps across the yard.

'Grandma!' A sturdy young lad came rushing towards them and threw himself into his grandmother's arms. 'I didn't know you were coming?'

'Neither did I, my love,' Nancy replied with aplomb. 'It was a spur of the moment thing. I haven't seen you for a while and you're growing so fast I was frightened I wouldn't recognise you!'

Young Hugo laughed at her nonsense, and the awkward moment was eased.

'I was feeling a bit low. It gets lonely there in town on my own sometimes,' Nancy said in a quiet voice to Katie. 'I thought maybe a change of scene and the fresh air out here at the ranch would blow away the cobwebs. I hope it's all right? Just for a day or two? I don't want to be a nuisance…'

'Yes, of course,' Katie said tightly. 'Come in.'

But Nancy could clearly see her dismay. She quickly paid off the hired buggy that had brought her from town and followed Katie into the ranch house. It was obvious that Hugh had good cause for his concern. Katie had lost a lot of weight since Nancy had last seen her and it was plain to see that she was ill.

'If you'd like to come into the sitting room,' Katie said with a visible effort at hospitality, 'I'll get you a coffee and then I'll go and get your room ready.'

'You'll do no such thing,' Nancy told her with gentle firmness. 'I can see I've come at a bad time and I shouldn't be making more work for you. So since you're stuck with me, let me help. I'm family and I know where everything is. Bed-linen still in the big cupboard at the back, yes?'

Katie nodded unwillingly.

'For now, we'll get my bed made up,' Nancy said, 'and then we'll see how I can be a help to you, not a nuisance, while I'm here.'

'But you really shouldn't...' Katie began, tears in her eyes. 'You've come to visit...'

'My dear, I wouldn't dream of being the kind of visitor that burdens you with more work...' She studied Katie's drawn face. 'Maybe I can be of help to you instead.' Silently she sent a prayer winging heavenwards that Katie would understand the message, that having another woman in the house she could confide in would ease her distress.

Nancy leaned forward and kissed the girl's thin cheek.

'Go and sit down – or get on with whatever you were doing. You can tell me all about everything later.'

But Katie trailed after her to the linen cupboard and into the guest bedroom. As Nancy swiftly made up the bed, Katie made desultory attempts at helping, but it was obvious the girl had no energy and no enthusiasm for the task. When it was done, she slumped on the bed.

'It's no good,' Katie said, her eyes filling with tears. 'You wouldn't believe me if I said everything was all right. Would you?'

'No,' Nancy said, coming to sit beside her. 'So what's the matter?'

Piece by piece the story came out. Katie had found a lump in her breast. A small one. A cyst or something like that. Nothing to worry about. But it had not gone away. It had grown. And there had been other worrying changes.

'So what does your doctor say?' Nancy probed.

But Katie shook her head. She would not meet Nancy's eyes.

'I'm too frightened to go to the doctor,' she said. 'If it's...' She gulped. 'If it's what I think it is... I'm afraid they'll remove my breast... and I can't bear that. It would make me... It would change how Hugh sees me...' She looked up, eyes bright with tears. 'He thinks I'm beautiful. Silly man thinks I'm perfect! And if they removed my breast I wouldn't be...' She shook her head. 'I daren't let him touch me now. I don't want him to know. I fight with him so we're not close like that any more... Oh Nancy, what am I going to do? I'm wrecking our lives! But I'm so afraid!'

Nancy turned and enfolded the weeping girl in her arms.

'My dear, Hugh truly loves you and he will love you just the same whatever happens.' She smiled gently. 'Love that depends on physical beauty never changing wouldn't last the years! We all get old. Living leaves scars. We all have bumps and wrinkles and ugly marks. We're none of us the perfect young beautiful people on the outside that we were when we met our husbands – and neither are they! But by the grace of our Lord Jesus, maybe the people we are on the inside are *more* beautiful. And it's the inside beauty that matters.'

She paused and gazed lovingly into Katie's eyes.

'Hugh loves *you*, the real you. Yes, as a hot-blooded young man he was attracted to a beautiful body – but it is the you that you have become that continues to hold his love, the *inside* you that endures for ever. And that you is truly beautiful.'

'But...' Katie began.

'No buts,' Nancy said, shaking her head with a smile. 'And there is one other thing.'

'What?' Katie asked.

'When Hugh promised he would love you "for better and for worse", "in sickness and in health", he meant it and he'll stick to it – and you – through thick and thin. That's what real love does.' Nancy pressed her forehead to Katie's. 'Don't take that chance away from him. Don't shut him out. Let him love you truly whatever happens. He's a good man.'

'I know that...' Katie said. 'I hadn't thought...'

'I know,' Nancy said and kissed her forehead. 'Now let's go and get supper.' She paused. 'And tomorrow I'll come with you to the doctor's.'

Katie hesitated. She sat a moment on the bed, gazing into Nancy's eyes.

'And you'll tell Hugh about the lump,' Nancy added. 'Tonight.'

Katie bit her lip.

'For better, for worse...'

Katie blinked hard. The beginnings of new strength crept into her exhausted face. She stood up.

'Yes,' she said. 'Yes.'

CHAPTER 20

Doctor Anstruther had known Katie since she was a baby. He had delivered her and seen her through all the usual childhood scrapes and illnesses. He had been present as a friend of the family at her wedding to Hugh and in due time it was he who had helped bring young Hugo into the world.

Now as Katie poured out her worries, he looked across at Nancy settled beside Katie on the other side of his desk.

'I'm glad you got her to come in,' he said. He shook his head at Katie. 'It's not good to neglect these things. If it is...' He paused, his kindly eyes worried. 'If it's what you've been worrying about, then the sooner it's dealt with the better.' He sat back and smiled reassuringly at them. 'Nowadays, the results of treatment are excellent.' He patted Katie's hand. 'But I don't think there's anything to worry about. You're too young for this to be anything serious.'

'I'm thirty-one,' Katie said.

'Exactly,' Dr Anstruther said. 'It's more usual in women aged between forty and forty-five. I'll take a look at you and then we'll be sure. I think it's most likely to be a little cyst, or an abscess, and that's easily dealt with.'

Nancy helped Katie remove her things and waited while the doctor gently checked Katie's breast. She could see the concern growing in his face as he took in the puckered skin and noted the discharge.

'I'm not sure,' he told them slowly. 'I still think it could simply be an abscess but we'd better be sure.'

Katie nodded.

'I'd like to take a wee bit of tissue for testing. I think that would be best.' He looked across at Nancy. 'If you'll wait outside, I'll get my nurse to assist me and we'll get it sent off to the lab this very day. We'll get the results as soon as we can.'

'Chin up. It'll soon be over,' Nancy whispered as she bent to hug Katie before she left the room.

But the biopsy results when they came were not good. This time Hugh drove Katie into town and sat with her while Dr Anstruther broke the news to them.

'The results are not 100 per cent clear,' he said. 'But in the face of the possibilities, I think we really need to treat this as though they were.' He shook his head unhappily. 'I'm not prepared to take any risks with your life,' he added.

Katie gripped Hugh's hand tight.

'What do you recommend?' Hugh asked, trying for a calmness he did not feel.

'I think Katie should have a mastectomy, a radical mastectomy, so we make sure every trace of the cancer is removed.' And he explained how the lymph nodes under her arm, the pectoral muscles under her breast, as well as the breast itself would be removed.

Katie sat as if frozen.

'Katie?' Dr Anstruther said. 'My dear, if there was any other way I would tell you. This is extensive surgery. Radical surgery. But results show that this is the best way to deal with carcinoma of the breast. Better to lose a breast than your life.'

'Katie,' Hugh said, his eyes pleading with her. 'I don't want to lose you. If this is the only way, I say let's go for it. I know it's going to be hard on you but I'll be beside you every step of the way. I love you, my darling. I want many more years of loving you and this will not change my love for you. Be brave. You heard Dr Anstruther: this is our best chance...'

Katie looked from one to the other.

'Our best chance?'

Dr Anstruther nodded.

'Then let's do it,' Katie said, gripping Hugh's hand fiercely. 'Let's get on with it.'

'Well done,' Dr Anstruther said. 'The sooner, the better.'

CHAPTER 21

Wick, July 1939

Ruby let herself in to George's digs with her key and trod quietly up the stairs to his sitting room.

'George?' she asked hesitantly.

George was sitting at his ease by the fire, reading a newspaper. Now he looked up with displeasure.

'What are you doing here?' he demanded. 'I told you we had to be careful. If anyone saw you...'

Ruby laughed bitterly. 'It's a bit late for that now,' she said, flinging herself into the armchair on the other side of the cheerfully burning fire.

George put his newspaper down and glared at her.

'And just what do you mean by that?' he asked, dark eyes flashing with annoyance.

'I'm pregnant,' Ruby told him.

'So?'

'You're going to be a daddy,' she said. 'Congratulations.'

'Wait a minute,' George said. His eyes searched her face. 'Surely this child is as likely to be Bobby's as mine? Which means Bobby has to get a move on and marry you if he thinks you're expecting his child…'

His eyes darkened with cynicism. 'It should be me congratulating you,' he said. 'Clever girl.'

But Ruby shook her head. Her mouth turned down and worry clouded her eyes.

'No,' she said. 'I'm sorry, George, but that won't work. There is no way that the baby is Bobby's and Bobby will know that only too well.'

George raised a questioning eyebrow.

'Because Bobby is a good little boy who does not play naughty games, even with naughty girls like me,' she stated.

'You're joking?' George said disbelieving.

'Believe me,' Ruby said, huddling up to the fire. 'I've done everything I can, but he was brought up strict. Those Cormacks! They take their churchgoing seriously, not just for Sundays. They're real God-fearing folk.'

George snorted disparagingly but Ruby continued, 'They follow the rules… What the Bible says. And one of those rules is that you don't go to bed with someone before the wedding night. I can't get Bobby to break that rule, no matter how I try!'

'You'll have to,' George said flatly. 'The plan was for you to marry Bobby. We can't mess this up now.'

He stood up and began pacing round the room, thinking furiously.

'Wait a minute. Where's Bobby today?' he asked.

'He's away on one of his Territorial Army things,' Ruby said. 'Bobby says there's definitely going to be a war and the TA will be called up first. He's even looking forward to it!'

'That could help,' George said thoughtfully. 'But you'll need to get him to the altar and into bed before he goes.'

'But how? I've tried everything!' Ruby protested.

George spoke in a high-pitched sickly-sweet tone: '*Oh Bobby, you could be killed in this horrid war! How could I live without you! Let us be married before you go and I'll have one night of love to remember you by!*'

Ruby laughed, but then she said thoughtfully, 'Well, yes, that might work.'

'It has to work!' George ground out. He stood threateningly over her. 'Just get him to marry you before he goes off to this war – if there's going to be a war!'

'I'll try, George,' Ruby assured him. 'But what about you... If there's a war?'

'I have an Argentinian passport,' George said. 'Until my country declares war, I'm not involved. And even then, they don't know where I am so I won't be called up.'

'So with Bobby away...' Ruby began, her face brightening.

George grinned. 'Quite so. But get that wedding ring on your finger first!'

CHAPTER 22

Sunday, 3 September 1939

The Cormack family sat around the wireless in the living room, waiting for the Prime Minister's broadcast to the nation. Dressed in their Sunday best and ready to set out for church, they nonetheless, like so many others, wanted to hear for themselves what the Prime Minister had to say.

In moments, the familiar voice rang out: 'This morning the British Ambassador in Berlin handed the German Government a Final Note stating that, unless we heard from them by 11 o'clock that they were prepared at once to withdraw their troops from Poland, a state of war would exist between us.'

'I have to tell you,' Mr Chamberlain continued, 'that no such undertaking has been received, and that consequently this country is at war with Germany.'

Joyce gasped. For so long, so many people had been hoping for peace, praying for peace, and working for peace. Now all their hopes were dashed. She looked round at her family seated, motionless, listening intently, as the news sank in. Mum, Dad, Bobby, Danny. This terrible war would touch them all.

She saw her father squeeze her mother's shoulder reassuringly. Hannah reached up and patted his hand, managing a watery smile. Joyce was glad that at sixty-four, her father was too old to be conscripted, but it was a different matter for her brothers. They were young enough to be called up to serve their country.

She made herself listen to what Mr Chamberlain was saying now: 'You may be taking your part in the fighting services or as a volunteer in one of the branches of the Civil Defence. If so you will report for duty in accordance with the instructions you have received. You may be engaged in work essential to the prosecution of war for the maintenance of the life of the people… If so, it is of vital importance that you should carry on with your jobs.'

Bobby's eyes lit up. 'Well, that's me,' he said cheerfully. 'Part of the fighting services. I'll be off tomorrow.'

His Territorial unit, the 5th Battalion Seaforth Highlanders, recruited locally from men in Caithness and Sutherland, had already been warned that they would be among the first to leave.

'The lads at work said war was sure to come,' Danny said quietly.

'We'll soon sort that man Hitler out!' Bobby said. 'You maybe won't ever need to leave your books and come and join us!'

'I may have no choice,' Danny said. 'With conscription, I'll maybe be on your heels, brother!'

'I'll see you over there then!' Bobby said, laughing.

But Joyce saw the worried look that passed between her parents. Danny's health was not that robust. Surely his work at the local newspaper would keep him safely at home? People would need newspapers to keep them informed during this war. Danny's job had to be one of the safe ones?

Bobby rose. 'I'd better get home and tell Ruby. She wasn't feeling very well this morning. That's why she didn't come with me.'

He blushed. Ruby's announcement of her pregnancy had come fast on the heels of their hurried wedding.

'Now may God bless you all,' the voice from the wireless cut in. They quietened to hear Mr Chamberlain out.

'May He defend the right. It is the evil things that we shall be fighting against – brute force, bad faith, injustice, oppression and persecution – and against them I am certain that the right will prevail.'

As the Prime Minister's announcement drew to a close, heavy showers of rain began to beat upon the windows.

'Oh dear, look at that,' Joyce's mother fussed. 'We'll be soaked before we get to church!'

Joyce saw her father exchange that glance with his sons that said 'Women!' Getting wet was now the least of their worries. His experiences in Flanders in the Great War – the war to end all wars they had been told it was, Joyce thought wryly – and the scars he still bore spoke clearly of the cost of war to the ordinary soldier. But he had come home safe, and Joyce hoped desperately that her brothers would too.

'I think we need to get to church,' her father said, rising to his feet. 'I fear we have more need of the Lord than ever before.'

Her mother nodded, her face sad and worried.

Joyce was pleased to see her brother Bobby stoop to kiss her cheek.

'You mustn't worry, Mum!' he said. 'Dad came home safe and that was a different kind of war. We'll be fine!'

CHAPTER 23

In another sitting room in the town, the Prime Minister's voice faded as the wireless set was switched off.

George returned thoughtfully to his chair.

'I'd better get home,' Ruby said, rising from the armchair on the other side of the fireplace. 'He'll expect me to be there when he gets back.'

'What was the excuse this time?'

Ruby stretched and patted the barely visible bump that was the beginning of her pregnancy.

'Morning sickness!' She laughed. 'He'll believe anything I tell him.'

'Just as well,' George said.

'Yes, Daddy,' Ruby said with a grin. She settled on the arm of George's chair and leaned in to kiss him. 'And by tomorrow he'll be gone, off to fight this stupid war, and I'll be free to enjoy myself!'

George frowned. 'His parents will be watching,' he said. 'You'll still have to be careful.'

Ruby tossed her gleaming blonde hair.

'There's been no problem so far,' she said. 'I don't foresee any in the future.'

CHAPTER 24

Joyce's eyes were red with weeping, but she smiled bravely as she waved her brother on his way. She and her mother and Ruby, now Bobby's wife, stood amongst the sizeable crowd as the local lads proudly marched down the road in their uniforms to the railway station on the first stage of their journey south to the war.

Oh, let him come home safely, Joyce prayed. *Protect him, Lord! He's my big brother and I love him so much! Please!*

The girl standing next to her looked at the pale lips moving silently. Let her pray, Ruby thought. It would not make a jot of difference. She did not believe in that sort of thing. You had to make your own life. Grab what you wanted with both hands. She and George were like peas out of the same pod in the way they thought. She hid a smile. With George she had certainly grabbed what she wanted and, to her delight, had got what she wanted.

She turned the brand-new wedding ring on her finger. It had not been easy but she had managed to get Bobby to the altar and acceptance that the babe to come was his. He had been a bit shamefaced in front of his family, but his mother had been matter-of-fact in her acceptance of the situation.

'It's not the first time and it won't be the last,' she had said as she had welcomed Ruby into the family.

The arrangements for the wedding were understandably rushed, but both Bobby's parents appeared to be willing to support her.

'I'd really like to keep my job for a while yet,' Ruby told them. 'In the office I'll be sitting down most of the time so I won't be tiring myself. And it would stop me getting lonely with Bobby being away.'

Mr Cormack had nodded unwillingly. It really was not the custom for married women to work, let alone when pregnant.

Innocently Joyce had come to her rescue. 'We do need Ruby,' she told her father. 'And she knows the work.'

He had shaken his head but then capitulated. 'Well, all right. But just for a little while.'

'And if you get tired, or don't feel well, you can just come through to the house,' Mrs Cormack offered.

Ruby had hidden a smile. It was all as George had said it would be. One foot in the Cormack door and she was already benefiting.

'I'm sure I'll be fine,' she had tried to protest and, as she had expected, Mr Cormack was having none of it.

'You mustn't worry about anything. With Bobby away, we'll look after you.'

And that was exactly what George had planned. It had been a little more difficult to maintain her independence in light of Bobby going off to the war. Mr Cormack had fretted about how she would manage on her own as her pregnancy progressed, especially since her mother did not live in Wick but fourteen miles away to the south in the village of Lybster.

'You'll be better staying with us till Bobby comes back,' his mother had said, assuming that she would fall in with her plans. But Ruby was having none of that. It would mean being in full view of the

Cormacks at all times, not to mention sharing a room with Joyce, and that would not suit!

'That's very kind of you,' she had said sweetly. 'But you don't want a crying baby in the house! Poor Joyce, she'd never get any sleep! No, I think I'll just stay where I am during the week but I'll go home to my mum at weekends.'

The flat in Dempster Street that Bobby had found for them was convenient and private enough for George to visit her, Ruby thought with a satisfied smile. And with her job in the office secure until the baby was born, she would see him every day.

And Joyce, of course. She had managed to get out of sharing a bedroom with Joyce, but she had to share the office with her. Ruby had to admit it rankled to have to watch the progress of George's romance with Joyce. She had to remind herself sternly that it meant nothing to him. Joyce was simply his meal-ticket, as Bobby was hers.

She saw Joyce dabbing her eyes as the stamp of marching feet died away.

'I think we all need a cup of tea, don't you agree?' Hannah Cormack suggested and gathered up the two girls as if they were the best of friends.

I can play this game, Ruby thought. *It will be worth it in the end.*

CHAPTER 25

Canada, 1939

Far away in Manitoba in Canada, Hugh sat with his mother listening to the news from Europe on the radio.

'This is terrible,' Nancy commented. 'War. Again. How dreadful. All those young men marching away to their deaths.'

Hugh listened thoughtfully. Would Canada be drawn into the fray like last time? He had been too young to fight in the last war and now at 40 was perhaps a little too old.

'Do you think it will affect us much?' Nancy began.

Hugh shook his head uncertainly. 'I don't know. I shouldn't think I'll get called up. They'll take the young ones first.' He sighed. 'And I'll guess some of the young ones will think it a fine adventure.'

'Yes. I'm glad.' Nancy caught herself. 'I'm not glad for them – going to their deaths! Or their mothers waiting and worrying at home. But I'm glad you won't be going.'

'Going where?'

They looked up. Katie had come silently into the room and was standing like a wraith, leaning her thin body against the doorframe.

Nancy and Hugh exchanged glances.

'Nothing for you to worry about,' Hugh began in calm measured tones.

'Nothing to worry about!' Katie flung the words back to him in sudden anger. 'That's fine for you to say – when we all know there's plenty to worry about!'

She pushed herself upright and came into the room, where she threw herself into an armchair, her eyes blazing out of her pale face.

'I'm not getting better and we all know it, but the pair of you skirt around it!' She gestured to herself. 'I've got eyes in my head! I can see I'm not well, and I need you to help me now, not pretend everything's all right!'

Hugh got up and went to kneel by her chair. He took her hand. 'I'm sorry, Katie love. Yes, of course we can see but we didn't know how you wanted us to deal with it.'

Tears pooled in Katie's eyes.

'I need you to be strong for me,' she whispered. 'And I need you to be honest with me too. So I can face this *with* you – not on my own, with you two pretending!'

'Shall we give Dr Anstruther another visit?' Nancy suggested. 'A check-up to see how you really are?'

Katie laughed, a horrid hollow sound.

'I don't need Dr Anstruther to tell me I'm ill.'

'But maybe he can help us…' Nancy's voice tailed off at the anger in Katie's eyes.

'Tell us how long I've got?'

'Katie!' Hugh said, shocked.

She kissed his forehead gently. 'I'm ill, Hugh, and I don't seem to be getting better, despite the operation.' She looked from Hugh to Nancy. 'The surgery was Dr Anstruther's best try. It hasn't worked. And now I'm not sure I'm going to make it.'

There. It was out in the open.

'My dear...' Nancy began.

But Katie silenced her with a look.

'No pretending,' she demanded. 'No more pretending. Speak only the truth to me. That's the only way we'll get through this.'

She fixed them with her eyes till they gave her the nod of agreement she wanted.

'I'm not afraid of death,' she said quietly. Her eyes were clear and shining as she spoke. 'I believe our Lord Jesus Christ died for my sins and that when I die I'll go to join Him in heaven and there's a lovely banquet waiting for me to enjoy and great singing to join in!' She grinned. 'Dancing too! And lots of old friends.' She shook her head. 'No, what comes *after* doesn't worry me at all.' She paused. 'It's the getting there.' And her eyes were worried now. 'I'm afraid of the pain. I'm afraid of it being horrible. And I'm afraid of the not knowing.'

Hugh and Nancy sat in silence, then Hugh said gently, 'All the more reason for a visit to Dr Anstruther. Let's see if we can get some of the information you need.'

CHAPTER 26

The visit to Dr Anstruther was as sad and as difficult as Hugh feared.

'I'm sorry,' he told them. 'I don't know. I really don't know... except that it's in the Lord's hands.'

And with that they had to be satisfied.

'I will do everything I can,' he assured them. 'You must call me when you need help.' He looked sternly at Katie. 'And you must accept the help you need.'

So when Hugh and Katie called on Nancy at her little house in town to retrieve young Hugo before they went home, it was Katie who asked her for help.

'Please,' she said. 'Come and stay with us. I don't want to worry my own mother. She's got her life with Dad in Calgary. But if you were willing... The ranch was your home. You know your way around. It would be a great help.'

And so, gently and gradually, Nancy once more took over the reins of the ranch household as the last remaining roses in Katie's cheeks paled and faded, and the cancer worked its way through her system. Mama Marie's healer cousin, old Christine, came to call, but her remedies could do little but ease the pain.

'What are we going to do?' Hugh begged his mother after one terrible night when Katie's suffering seemed unbearable.

In answer, Nancy spent hours sending ever-more desperate prayers up to a God who seemed able only to grieve with them. Heart-sore, Nancy threw herself into doing whatever she could to keep Hugh and young Hugo fed and clean. Hard work always seemed to help keep the fear at bay, at least for a little while.

'Why doesn't God make my mummy better?' Hugo demanded one afternoon.

Nancy caught Hugh's eye. Neither of them had an answer for him.

'I don't know, my love,' Nancy said. 'Sometimes bad things happen that we just don't understand – can't understand.'

But Hugo had stood up and announced, 'Then I don't like God if He won't make my mummy better.'

After he had gone out, Hugh turned to his mother and said ruefully, 'I'm not sure I like God very much at the moment. What has Katie ever done wrong? She doesn't deserve this! Why does it have to be her?' His voice rose with pent-up emotion.

'I don't know, my love,' Nancy said, realising that her only answer was the same as she had offered her grandson.

'But I love her so much!' Hugh burst out. 'And I'm so frightened of losing her! How can God part us when we should have all the rest of our lives ahead of us? I need her here with me! Hugo needs her! How can God do this to us?'

He covered his face with his hands.

'I know, my love,' Nancy began. 'But...'

Hugh stood up, the anger clear in his face. 'Oh, don't give me that "If it's God's will" stuff! What kind of a God would ever do this to perfectly innocent people? No kind of God I'd want anything to do with!'

97

And he slammed out of the room and stalked across the yard. A few moments later Nancy saw him lead a horse out of the stable. She sighed. Perhaps a ride out in the clear crisp air would help him. It seemed she could not.

She had no answers. But she remembered Mama Marie saying 'When you have no answers, God does. And you'll find them in His Word.' She stood and went over to the bookcase and reached down Marie's battered old Bible. She stroked the well-worn black cover gently.

'Hugh's right, You know,' she spoke softly to God. 'If You sent bad things, You wouldn't be the kind of God I'd want anything to do with either!'

Tears came to her eyes as the sorrow and grief flooded through her.

'Heavenly Father, *our* Father, I pray for mercy,' Nancy prayed. 'I pray for Your love and mercy for our lovely Katie and for Hugh and Hugo. You are the Giver of Life. And yes, I know, it is your prerogative not only to give it, but to take it away too. And I will say the rest of that verse, even though it's hard: Blessed, Lord, be Your Name.'

She sighed. Where would she find words of comfort? Was it comfort she needed? With conscious irony she opened the Bible at the Book of Job, and saw on the page before her the verse she had just quoted. Chapter 1 verse 21: '*The Lord gave, and the Lord hath taken away; blessed be the name of the Lord.*' The words had been spoken by Job after all his wealth had been destroyed and his children had been killed. Surely he knew a thing or two about blessing and loss.

As did she, she thought. God had given her so much and so graciously. First the amazing gift of Hugh. And in Hugh, so many other lovely gifts, not least his beloved Katie and their son, Hugo, growing up strong and healthy. There had been much joy, much delight over the years. God had been very good to them.

But yes, He had also taken away. Marie and Bill had lived to a good old age before He called them home. Home to their Lord. Though there was sadness, there was also much comfort in that. Later, the Lord had taken her beloved Clem and though she missed him dreadfully, she knew the parting was only temporary. They would be reunited one day.

She had known blessing and loss, and now she needed to support Hugh and Hugo as they faced the loss of Katie. However long it would take, it would be a shadow hanging over them.

It would be hard – for Hugh especially.

'Dearest Lord,' Nancy prayed, 'please keep Hugh close to You. Don't let him lose his faith in You. I know he has a choice in this: to turn away from You in his pain and anger, or run to You for the comfort and peace only You can give. I pray that he will turn to You. I know You wait with Your arms open wide – for both him and Katie. Oh please make her passing easy, as gentle, as kindly as possible. It is torture for us to watch what she is going through. Oh I beg You, grant her and us Your peace.'

CHAPTER 27

Wick

The autumn morning was cold and grey, but Joyce's heart was lit by an inward glow as she sat at her dressing table, carefully removing the pins from her hair. Not so very long ago, she thought with amusement, she would not have bothered. After all, today was just another day at work. Yes, she would have dressed quite smartly, as usual, but she would not have taken this much trouble.

She smiled at her reflection in the mirror. It was so different now. And all because of her darling George. He would be there, in and out of the office all day, and she wanted to look her best for him.

How lovely being in love was! It made her eyes sparkle and gave her a radiance that was quite unmistakable. She had seen it in other girls but never in herself before. She was sure, if they could see her now, her friends would nudge one another and tease, 'She's in love!' And it was true. There was something about being in love that just could not be hidden.

Joyce sighed with contentment. Even better was that her parents had realised just what a lovely person George was. She had overheard them talking in the kitchenette the other evening after supper.

'He's been a great help since Bobby left for the war,' her father said. 'I'll give him that.'

Joyce heard the chink of crockery as her mother finished the washing-up.

'I'm glad.' There was a pause and another chink. 'Without Bobby...'

'Aye, it's not so easy. And now some of the other men have gone too, I'm needing all the help I can get.'

'It's good he's making himself useful.'

'Oh, he's doing that!' Her father laughed. 'It seems he can turn his hand to anything! It was a happy day for us when he turned up!'

'It was for Joyce,' her mother put in quietly.

'She does seem happy.'

'Oh, she is.' Joyce could hear the smile in her mother's voice.

'Well, I hope he'll treat her right,' her father said gruffly. There was a pause and then a low murmur. 'Oh Hannah, I wish I'd had more sense. I wasted so many years I could have shared with you. I'm so sorry...'

'We're doing fine now,' her mother said. 'And we'll have plenty more years to enjoy, God willing. We've got Joyce and the boys. The business is going well. Our health is good. Our life is good. God has been very good to us.'

'Aye,' her father agreed. 'But this war...'

Joyce had gone into the kitchenette then.

'I'm happy to continue working in the office,' she assured them. 'It's a reserved occupation, so at least you won't lose me.'

'You're a good girl,' her father said.

'And it's good that George is Argentinian,' Joyce added. 'He won't be called up till his country joins in the war, and he says that's unlikely.'

'That's right,' her father had agreed. 'I don't know what I'd do without him now.'

As Joyce finished brushing her hair till it shone, she felt a sudden pang. She did not know how she could bear life without George now. But she supposed one day he would have to go away – either to fight in this horrid war or go back to his home in Argentina. Could she see herself returning to Argentina with him? She was not at all sure that she could bear to leave her parents.

She sighed. It was a horrid tangle. Was there to be no future for their love?

They would just have to make the most of the present, she decided robustly – like so many others. Seize life while it was there. Enjoy what they had.

Carefully she dressed and checked her appearance. Yes, though she said it herself, she looked nice. And she could cope with her mother's knowing gaze at breakfast.

It was worth it. Because George was worth it.

CHAPTER 28

Ruby tried to ease her aching back. The hard chair behind her desk in the office did her no favours and she was longing for the end of the day when she could get home to the flat and put her feet up. Getting no relief from her wrigglings, she rose and stretched and wandered towards the counter.

The door from the street opened and George breezed in. He was, as always, nattily dressed in his dark blue suit and crisp white shirt, his thick black hair sleeked back with brilliantine. Ruby smiled with pleasure as she feasted her eyes on him. He twirled his chauffeur's cap round in his hand as he stepped into the waiting area in front of the counter.

As Ruby began to speak, George suddenly signalled her to silence with a warning glower. As if on cue, the door from the adjoining house opened and Joyce, her hair freshly waved, her eyes sparkling, came through.

At once George pushed open the door into the office and, walking through, took both Joyce's hands in his and kissed her cheek.

'*Cariño*,' he whispered.

Ruby bridled. He never called her sweet names like that! What did it mean anyway? She would have to find out. But George had sensed her reaction and again shot a warning glare her way. Ruby banged the cash drawer under the counter, making the coins jangle together loudly. Joyce blushed and hurried to her desk at the back of the room. George lounged against the wall, watching them both.

Ruby winced as her back twinged again, but she was determined not to give in and leave the way clear for Joyce to have George all to herself day in and day out. She would stick it out as long as she could.

'Ah, George.' It was Mr Cormack who had let himself quietly into the office from the house. He had a sheet of paper in his hand and was studying it carefully.

'I see we've got Sandy Ross's funeral this morning, then there's a hire to Thrumster in the afternoon. Taking Mrs Dunnet's daughter and the grandchildren out to see her.' He paused. 'Go easy on the pedal, George,' he cautioned. 'The petrol rationing is beginning to bite.'

'Yes, *señor*,' George said. He straightened up and sent both girls a smile. Then, placing his cap on his shining head, he left the office.

Rab Cormack watched him go. Ruby tried to still the urge to ease her back, but a particularly sharp twinge made her wince and she saw to her annoyance that it had not escaped Mr Cormack's notice.

'Ruby, my dear,' Rab said, 'I'm not happy about you going on working so many long hours. I know you young women do things differently than in my day, but I do think maybe you should be taking more rest.'

'I'm fine,' Ruby protested. 'Thank you, Mr Cormack. Really, I'm fine.' But as she tried to settle her back she could not suppress another wince.

Rab came over and put a kindly hand on her shoulder.

'Now, there's no need for that,' he said firmly. 'You don't *have* to work. I'll make sure you've got enough money while Bobby's away. Why don't you take a few days off and see how you feel when you've had a chance to put your feet up and rest?'

Ruby began to protest but Rab was having none of it.

'I tell you what,' he said. 'I'll get George to run you out to your mother's in Lybster and you can let her look after you for a few days. It will do you good.'

Ruby glanced wildly at Joyce, who was nodding and smiling.

'That's a good idea, Ruby,' Joyce said. 'It can't be nice for you all alone in the flat – and having to go up and down those stairs every day! It will be much nicer for you to be at your mother's. She'll cosset you and look after you!'

And I'll be out of your way, Ruby thought crossly.

She looked from one to the other of the Cormacks, father and daughter. All goodwill and smiles. Thinking only of what was best for her. Oh yes. If only they knew! Sending her to her mother in Lybster would take her away from the only thing that mattered in her life – George! And with petrol rationing he would not be able to get out to see her. The flat in Dempster Street had been convenient in more ways than one!

But the Cormacks were determined.

'Would you like Joyce to give you a hand with packing?' Mr Cormack offered. 'Why don't you take enough for a week or two, and see how you get on?'

His generosity grated. Why couldn't he mind his own business?

Ruby swallowed hard and forced out a smile, remembering to include Joyce in its false beam.

'That's very kind of you,' she said. 'But I'm sure I'll manage. I'm not ill!'

105

'No,' Rab Cormack said. 'But you should take care.'

Ruby managed to suppress the bile that rose in her throat as she observed Joyce's satisfaction.

She would take care. Of George. She would make sure of that.

CHAPTER 29

1940

The baby was born in February to the usual counting on fingers and head-shaking among the old biddies. Ruby ignored them all. She was pleased and relieved to see that Amanda, with her dark eyes and downy dark-brown hair, could as easily be taken for Bobby's child as George's, so there was no problem there.

Ruby would have preferred a little more appreciation of the baby from her real father. It had taken George long enough to appear at her mother's in Lybster after the birth and when he arrived, he had dismissed the infant with the disdainful comment: 'A girl!'

'George!' Ruby protested. 'She's your daughter – your first child.' But it made no difference.

'Should you not have called her Robertina? After Bobby? Surely that's what they'd expect!' George demanded. 'That's the local way, is it not? Take the father's name and make it female?'

'Like mine,' Ruby said with a rueful laugh. 'I'm Reubina really. My Dad was Reuben.' She shook her head. 'No, I wasn't going to do that to any child of mine. And anyway...' She tried a coaxing smile. 'I thought it would be nice – a little secret between us. Amanda. It means...'

'I know what it means,' George grated 'But it will not do. It would not do for people to get… any ideas. You understand?'

It was not a question but an instruction and there was a warning behind it. Ruby knew not to cross George so she nodded.

'Yes, yes, of course,' she said quickly. Calling the child Amanda was risk enough. 'I understand. But it's too late now. She's registered Amanda Cormack. I'm sorry. I just wasn't thinking…'

'Women,' George said disparagingly. 'Well, thinking's my job. You just stay here with your mother a little longer and play your part till Bobby gets home. It will all turn out exactly as we have planned.'

He had grinned then, a broad wolfish grin that she had come to hate. It spoke of his plans working out as he wished – and that meant his relationship with Joyce Cormack.

Ruby ground her teeth but determinedly kept silent. It was better by far that she was out here at her mother's than seeing them together every day. She hated having to watch George's skilful courtship of that girl who did not deserve him.

But George had caught her mood. He took her by the shoulders and shook her roughly.

'Now, let us have none of this. You know what is at stake. Our future, yes?'

He waited till Ruby lowered her eyes and nodded her acquiescence.

'Our time will come,' he assured her. He kissed the top of her head and smiled into her eyes. 'In the meantime, we can take advantage of every opportunity…'

His conspiratorial grin soothed Ruby's anxiety. George had become adept at inventing hires to the places around Lybster, tucking the big black car away where it would not be seen and spending an hour with her. She knew he was also picking up the alcohol that was illegal in still-dry Wick and therefore a lucrative and desirable product, but she told herself that was just an extra benefit. She was the main reason for his trips. Her mother had accepted the arrangement without question and would whisk the baby away 'for a walk' whenever George appeared at the door.

Though the folk in Lybster were aware of the German planes that flew so frequently over Caithness *en route* to drop their bombs on Scapa Flow or Wick Aerodrome, the village itself was little troubled – unlike Wick itself. There, air raid warnings were a regular occurrence, as were the funerals of airmen and sailors which provided plentiful work for Rab Cormack's ambulances and hearse.

News was closely censored and the local weekly newspapers, *The John O'Groat Journal* and *The Caithness Sentinel*, on which folk depended for official information, were pared down from eight pages to four. Without George to keep her informed of everything that was really going on, Ruby would have found her enforced exile at her mother's unbearable.

When an enemy Heinkel was pursued back to Wick by a flight of Hurricanes and landed at the aerodrome rather than ditch in the sea, there was huge excitement as the two survivors were taken down to the police cells for the night. What they said when served tea that evening, how they looked – so young, smart-looking, well-dressed… George brought every snippet to entertain Ruby.

But as the air activity over Wick increased with flights of Hudsons continuously in the air and flashes of gunfire sometimes low in the sky, sometimes high, as the battle for air supremacy and to protect Scapa Flow continued, the novelty began to wear off.

As did Ruby's pleasure in her new daughter. She had thought the baby would bind George closer to her, but his reaction to the child put paid to that hope. Seeing him once or twice a week – and always unpredictably, unexpectedly – meant she had to be looking her best at all times, and her mother ready and willing to go out and take the child with her.

Joyce Cormack, of course, was deemed to be in a reserved occupation – manning the office at the garage. While Ruby was trapped out in Lybster, Joyce was seeing George every day – and George, no doubt, would be taking advantage of every opportunity there.

Ruby paced the floor with her crying baby. This was not what she had planned for her life. How unfortunate that married women were excluded from being called up for war work!

Surely she could do better than this?

CHAPTER 30

Joyce gazed up into George's eyes. He was so very handsome. And he's chosen *me*, she thought with wondering delight.

Joyce had been walking out with George for several months now. He had taken her for walks and to country dances, always checking with her parents for their permission. Joyce loved his old-fashioned foreign ways. He was such a gentleman!

Her mind was so aflutter she had to concentrate to hear what he was saying.

'So I wondered… this evening…'

'Yes?' she prompted breathlessly. She knew she would agree to anything he suggested. And with a tiny guilty shiver, she acknowledged the depth of wickedness in that revealing truth. *Anything?* Yes, she acknowledged silently to herself. Anything.

The door from the house opened, startling them. George stepped back, allowing Joyce to see that it was her mother who had come through.

Joyce stood up.

'Mother!' she said in surprise.

The office – like the garage and the workshop – was her father's domain and her mother seldom intruded. As Joyce focused on her mother she saw that her eyes were red from weeping and she held an envelope and a small square of paper in her hand. A telegram. Joyce's eyes flew from the telegram to her mother's face, then back again.

She stepped rapidly towards her mother, picking up on her distress.

'Oh no!' Joyce cried out in fear. 'Mum, what is it? Who is it? Is it Bobby? Or Danny? Has one of them been wounded?' But she saw the terrible answer in her mother's anguished face and threw herself into her mother's arms. 'Oh no!'

'George,' her mother said steadily as she held Joyce tightly. 'Please would you go out to the garage and get Mr Cormack.'

Joyce felt George's gentle touch on her shoulder as he went past her and out of the office.

'Mum?' Joyce whispered. 'Tell me? Who is it?' She gulped. She could not bear to hear the news.

'It's Bobby,' her mother said quietly. 'He's been killed in action.'

'Show me.' Her father's voice.

Joyce stepped away and watched her mother hand the dreadful document to her father. He stood, tall and straight, his face sombre as he scanned the few terrible words on the telegram. She saw his shoulders slump as the grief hit him. Before her eyes, her father seemed to age in that moment. Then he steadied, folded the paper and put it in his wallet, placing the wallet carefully in the inside pocket of his jacket.

He looked at Joyce and her mother and opened his arms to encompass them both, folding them into his embrace. George stood awkwardly outside the little circle, watching.

'Good Lord, I pray You have our boy safe with You now, where he will suffer no more pain or hurt,' Rab Cormack prayed aloud over the bowed heads of his wife and his daughter. 'And may we one day be reunited with him and with You.' He paused and swallowed hard. 'And give us strength to go on without him.' He bent his head to kiss first Joyce's cheek, then her mother's. All three faces were wet with tears.

'You loved him,' Rab Cormack said to his wife. 'Like a mother. Always. You were the mother he should have had. You stepped in and more than filled that gap.' His smile was full of sorrow, but love shone through the pain. 'Thank you for that. I will never be able to thank you enough...'

Hannah stood on tiptoe and put her finger on his lips.

'No need,' she said. 'I've been repaid in full – and more than full – every day of my life since he was born. He has always been a delight to me. I was happy to be a mother to him. He brought me joy. And he brought me you.' Words failed as the memories flooded through. Hannah's tears flowed freely, mingling sorrow and joy.

Joyce leaned over to kiss her mother's cheek. She knew how much her mother had loved Bobby even though he was not her natural-born son. The product of Rab's brief and unhappy marriage to her mother's sister Belle who had died in childbirth, the infant had been taken on by Hannah, and she had brought him up and loved him. And Joyce had loved him too. Her big brother.

They stood as if frozen in their thoughts, then her father roused himself.

'Someone will have to tell Ruby.'

'Tell Ruby what?' a bright voice enquired and all four heads turned to gaze at the cheerful apparition that had appeared in their midst.

'Well?' Ruby demanded, dropping her handbag on the counter and pulling off her gloves. 'What's going on?' She looked up at the four faces staring at her, taking in the startled expressions, the tears.

'Ruby...' Joyce's mother began.

'What is it?' Ruby asked, warily now.

'It's Bobby,' Joyce's father began. 'I'm terribly sorry, my dear. We've just heard... He's been killed in action.' He reached in his pocket for his wallet, carefully opened it and drew out the telegram. He held it out to her. 'I'm sorry, my dear, but Bobby won't be coming home. He's dead.'

Ruby rapidly scanned the words on the telegram, then she stopped and forced herself to read it again. She could feel the eyes of the Cormacks and of George on her. Determinedly, she schooled her face to expressionlessness, but her heart fizzed with joy. This was wonderful news, the best possible news!

I'm free! I'm free!

The words filled her mind as Ruby felt the heavy weight of her loveless marriage to Bobby Cormack roll from her shoulders. She thought of the poor fumbling, adoring man she had thought herself inextricably bound to for the foreseeable future. How often she had wondered how she could keep from telling him exactly what she thought of him and his sanctimonious family, and then getting out, no matter what it cost. Except she knew that it would cost her George – and that was a price she was not willing to pay. She was not willing to lose George.

She thought quickly. She was a widow now. Bobby would not be coming back. She was completely at liberty to continue her liaison with George.

Then a new thought struck her – quick and hot and sharp and sudden: she was single now. She was free to *marry* George! And that

114

was what she wanted. That plain-Jane Joyce Cormack would never have him!

Ruby suppressed the smile of triumph that threatened to erupt. For now, she would have to bide her time. Play the tragic young war widow. Get all she could get from the Cormacks while they were feeling bad about Bobby's death.

Yes. This could be very much to her advantage.

By the time she raised her eyes to the waiting gazes of the Cormacks, she was ready. She had found a handkerchief in her pocket and used it to cover her face.

'Oh!' she cried in a broken voice. 'Oh no!' and she went limp and slumped to the ground, allowing the Cormacks to rush around and fuss about her.

Yes, Ruby thought, as she listened to their concerned voices. She could do very nicely from this.

CHAPTER 31

George alone did not rush to Ruby's assistance. His eyes narrowed as he watched her artistic performance. Her eyes fluttered open, lace-edged handkerchief held to them, as she uttered little broken cries, and allowed Mr Cormack to help her to a chair.

Joyce and Mrs Cormack fussed around Ruby, their grief and shock almost forgotten in their attempts to calm and comfort her. George just hoped she would not lay it on so thick that even the Cormacks would see through her.

But he had to admit she was making a good job of it. He stood to one side, his mind racing. How would this news affect him and his plans?

With Bobby dead, who would the family business now go to? Bobby's half-brother, Danny, was next in line. If he were to come home safely from the war.

But Danny had no interest in cars and engines. He was a man of ink and words. He had served his apprenticeship as a typesetter and printer at the *Caithness Sentinel* before being called up. No, if Danny returned, he would not want to change horses and work in the garage with his father.

George pursed his lips as he thought, and caught Joyce's swift, concerned glance. He managed a gentle, reassuring smile, making his face appropriately sad. She returned his smile hesitantly.

Ah yes, he thought. There was Joyce. She loved the family business. She loved the cars and the work with the public. She threw herself into organising wedding cars, and even took pleasure in arranging funerals. 'For the family's sake,' she used to say. George thought her a strange creature to be so involved in such things rather than the frivolous interests of other young women of her own age, but now he began to see that he could put it to his advantage.

Swiftly, George assessed the cards that remained in his hand. There was in fact only one – and that was Joyce. He would have to marry her and that as soon as possible. Then he would need to persuade Rab Cormack that he and Joyce could manage the business between them. Let him see them operating as a competent team and, before much longer, the old man would be willing to leave it all in their capable hands. He would soon find a way to sideline Joyce and then he would have his hands on what he wanted.

Ruby suddenly threw him a swift calculating glance from above the lace-edged handkerchief. He gave her a level stare. He was not going to permit her to queer his pitch.

But, he thought, once he had everything the way he wanted – dear little Joyce pregnant and married – and yes, it had to be in that order to ensure her father would let them marry – yes, with Joyce safely tucked away at home, he would be free to run the business the way he wanted.

George considered the opportunities. He could increase the whisky runs in from the country, add in some interesting black-market products – and still have time to enjoy the delights that Ruby offered.

Unobserved by the others, he winked slyly at Ruby, catching her quick grin of understanding before the mask of grief and the lace-edged handkerchief were swiftly replaced.

CHAPTER 32

Joyce began tidying up the office. It was past half-past four and it would soon be time to shut up shop and go next door to the house to get ready. As she worked, she thought about that evening's promised treat. George had been so sweet since her brother's death and she was pleased that even her parents had accepted that they were officially walking out together. Tonight he had suggested they go to the cinema.

The low roar of enemy aircraft overhead and the answering firing of the gunner at the South Head battery was so familiar now that Joyce barely paid attention. But then there came an explosion so loud – the loudest she had ever heard. Her mother came rushing into the office.

'What was that? What's happened?'

They hurried outside to join other folk coming out of nearby buildings to see what was going on.

'Look!'

Someone pointed and all eyes turned. From the direction of the harbour, a pall of black smoke was rising.

The telephone in the office rang. Joyce ran back and answered it.

'Yes, yes, of course. At once.'

She hurried back outside and into the garage.

'George, the ambulance. Bank Row has been hit – and there are lots of casualties.'

George thrust his cap on his head and hurried to get the ambulance down to the scene of the attack.

'Nothing more we can do out here,' Hannah said, putting an arm round her daughter's shoulders.

'Oh Mum, it's terrible!' Joyce cried. 'They said people had been killed.'

Rab Cormack had joined them. Now he and his wife exchanged sad glances.

'That's the way of war, my dear,' he said.

'But it's one thing when it's soldiers,' Joyce protested. 'They're meant to be in the middle of fighting. Innocent civilians in their own homes going about their own business are different!'

And her horror only increased when they discovered later that in this, the first daylight attack of the war on Great Britain, seven children had been killed.

'But children!' Joyce exploded. 'It's so wrong!'

The other eight who had lost their lives included three women. Houses and shops had been demolished and damaged, not only in Bank Row where two bombs had fallen within yards of each other, but also in neighbouring Rose Street.

George, who had seen the aftermath of gun battles in Chicago, was nevertheless shaken by what met his eyes when he arrived on the scene.

'Carnage,' he said briefly, when on his return to the garage, Joyce and her parents plied him with questions. 'There were dead and injured lying about on the street. And the destruction!

Windows torn out of the houses and smashed to pieces. Shocking.'

He had been among those helping remove the injured to the Bignold Hospital on the northern edge of town.

'Pretty well non-stop,' he reported. 'They'll be hard put to cope with so many at once.'

But they heard later that extra volunteer doctors and women who were formerly trained nurses had turned out to assist.

'Stay for tea,' Hannah had said to him. 'I don't think Joyce wants to go out tonight.'

'I don't think I could go out and enjoy myself...' Joyce said.

'I understand, cariño,' George said. 'Thank you, Mrs Cormack.'

The family meal was a subdued business. George was uncharacteristically quiet and Joyce was still shocked by this attack on her home town.

'I'll maybe have a wander down and take a look,' Rab said when they had finished their meal. He looked to George.

'If you'll excuse me, I will not accompany you,' George said. 'I have already seen...'

'Yes, of course.'

Rab rose. 'Terrible things happen in wars,' he said, with a sigh. 'It's the way of it.'

He went to get his coat and hat and then they heard the front door close behind him.

'Thank you for the food,' George said politely to Hannah. He turned to Joyce. 'Perhaps we'll see that film another time?'

She managed a watery smile. He was so thoughtful.

'I shall see you at work tomorrow,' he said, his eyes smiling gently into hers. 'Good night.' And he took his leave.

'He is very nice,' Joyce said quietly.

Her mother raised an eyebrow.

'And sensitive.' Hurriedly Joyce added, 'The way he was affected by what he saw down at Bank Row. He's got feelings.'

'Mmm,' her mother said. 'Yes, it certainly shook him.' She stood up. 'Let's get the washing-up done before your father comes back.'

CHAPTER 33

George walked thoughtfully back to his lodgings. The devastation in Bank Row had hit him hard. This little grey town out on the edge of nowhere should have been one of the safest places on earth in this stupid war.

But no. It was in direct line of the Germans' bombing raids on the hugely important naval base at Scapa Flow. Wick had been ahead of its time in having an aerodrome – an aerodrome which appeared so proudly on maps that the Germans knew there would be opposition there that needed to be dealt with.

The almost daily German reconnaissance flights were getting on his nerves. And today's attack… The sheer scale of the destruction and the death toll. Was nowhere safe?

George strode along unseeing, as his thoughts roiled round in his brain. It appeared that nowhere in Europe was safe.

There was no point going back to Glasgow. It was a prime target for the Luftwaffe.

The Atlantic blockade meant he could not get back to South America. And he was most definitely persona non grata in the United States of America.

'George?'

He came to with a start, almost at the door to his lodgings. The man who had accosted him was one of his regular customers for the supplies of illicit whisky he smuggled into town.

'Harry,' George ground out. 'What do you want? I don't think you're due another delivery just yet – unless you and your mates are drinking more than usual – and I wouldn't blame them!'

'What do *I* want?' Harry laughed. 'That's a fine way to talk to a man who was going to do you a good turn.'

'Oh yeah,' George said cynically, fishing in his pocket for his door key.

'Early night?' Harry enquired. 'No pretty lady to keep you company? I'd have thought the Wick girls would be so frightened tonight, a man like you would have your pick...'

George turned back from the door thoughtfully. Harry was right. Joyce's fear would surely have made her only too ready to fall into his arms... and his bed. As he castigated himself for missing the opportunity, he remembered Hannah Cormack's all-seeing grey eyes. No. With her mother there, there would have been no chance of seducing Joyce tonight.

But perhaps these raids could be turned to his advantage. The more raids, the more frightened Joyce would be. And the more frightened she was, the more likely she would be to turn to him. Yes. And now perhaps Wick was not such a bad place to be. This war and all the disadvantages he had been cursing just a moment before could all play into his hands and help his plans along. He smiled and confronted the man.

'Just say what you have to say, then you can go,' George said.

'That's not friendly,' Harry said. 'I just thought you might be interested in a new place that could be in need of your services... And on a night like tonight, there are a lot of nerves needing steadying, so if you have some supplies tucked away, you could do good business.'

'What's in it for you?' George demanded suspiciously.

The man shrugged. 'I fancied a game of cards and I was just wondering if you played?'

'Cards?'

'Poker.'

'Where?'

'This new place...'

George considered. An empty evening lay before him. Joyce was out of reach behind the impregnable shield of her mother's protection. Ruby was in Lybster. But Harry was offering an introduction to a new business opportunity – and a companionable game of cards.

There was no competition.

George smiled.

'Lead on,' he told Harry.

CHAPTER 34

The next raid, when it came, was much heavier. The Germans' main target was the aerodrome itself as three Heinkels flew low over the grey slate rooftops of the town, their machine-guns ablaze. A Saturday evening in late October, people were still about in the streets and many had lucky escapes from the machine-gun bullets that peppered the roads and buildings.

And when the planes dropped their high-explosive cargo, the series of loud explosions had everyone running for cover as the whole town seemed to vibrate with the impact.

'Where is it this time?' Hannah asked when Joyce returned from the garage where she had been giving the drivers their instructions.

'Hill Avenue,' Joyce said. 'The bombs landed short of the aerodrome, in Hill Avenue. One bungalow has been demolished, and there are folk killed and injured.'

They stood at the front window of the living room and watched the ambulances rush past.

'I expect George and your dad could do with something to eat when they get in,' Hannah said. With the shortage of able-bodied men to drive the vehicles, Rab Cormack had stepped in to take his share of the driving. Tonight both he and George were at the wheel of ambulances.

But the men did not return till very late. Hannah and Joyce tried to keep busy, but it was with huge relief that they heard the ambulances finally drive into the garage.

'I've brought George back with me,' Rab said as the two men stumbled in the door, grey with fatigue.

'I should think so. He looks as bad as you,' Hannah said, scolding gratefully, now that they had returned safely. 'Now sit yourselves down...'

Joyce went and sat on the arm of George's chair and squeezed his shoulder.

'Was it bad?' she whispered.

He closed his eyes. 'Not as bad as Bank Row. Not as many dead, or injured...'

'So why were you so long?' she asked curiously.

'A lot of the bombs didn't explode,' her father explained from his armchair beside the fire. 'So it wasn't safe for folk to stay in their houses.'

'And a lot of the houses were damaged,' George put in.

'Not just in Hill Avenue,' Rab said. 'In all the streets around – Henrietta Street, Rosebery Terrace, George Street...'

'So what happened to those people?' Hannah asked.

'We took them to the High School. The Civil Defence had arranged for emergency accommodation for them there. That's where they'll stay tonight.'

Rab looked across at George.

'Been a bit of a night.'

George nodded, his eyelids drooping with weariness.

Hannah snorted and handed out sandwiches and cups of tea.

'George, you must be exhausted,' she said. 'You can't go back to your lodgings on your own at this time. Would you like to stay here tonight? You'd be very welcome. There's the boys' bedroom...'

Joyce's eyes lit up with delight.

'Oh, say you will?' she breathed.

George considered. Was this the opportunity he had been waiting for? Surely Joyce's bedroom could not be far away?

'That's very kind of you, Mrs Cormack,' he began.

'Good man,' Rab said. 'I'm sure we've got some pyjamas that will fit you, and a razor...'

'Thank you.'

Rab yawned suddenly. It had been a long hard evening, and was now well past midnight.

'Time for everybody to go to bed,' Hannah announced, gathering up the used plates and teacups on a tray.

George tried to catch Joyce's eye but she was busy helping her mother.

'I'll show you where you'll be sleeping,' Rab said, climbing ponderously to his feet and leading the way out of the room.

George hid his amusement. If he had his way, and he fully intended to, he would be in Joyce's room. But when they got to the top of the stairs and Mr Cormack explained the layout of the upper floor, George looked about him in dismay.

The boys' bedroom, as the family called it, was at the far left-hand side of the house. Mr and Mrs Cormack's bedroom was right in the middle, with Joyce's bedroom tucked in on the other side of theirs.

His face lightened when he saw that the family bathroom was next to Joyce's room. There was his opportunity. An easy detour...

'We had the house altered for us a few years back,' Mr Cormack was saying. 'Put in a modern bathroom up here, the kitchenette downstairs, all to Mrs Cormack's specifications.'

Mrs Cormack had come upstairs and was returning from the airing cupboard with fresh towels.

She handed them over to George and laughed cheerfully. 'Only thing they never got right was the squeaky floorboards! We've got used to them but I hope they won't disturb you.'

Those grey eyes gleamed with warning humour as she looked at him, and George knew with a sinking heart that there would be no creeping around this house for him tonight.

CHAPTER 35

'I am so sorry! Truly!'

George threw out his hands in a delightfully foreign gesture of regret, but that only very slightly assuaged Joyce's disappointment. She had so been looking forward to an evening out with George. But now the promised treat had to be cancelled. She blinked back the sudden tears. It was a bitter blow. There was little fun these dark winter nights with the blackout and the rationing and the restrictions. And life seemed ever more precious, living in such dangerous times that you never knew when another attack would hit the town and who would be killed next.

Her eyes flew to George's. What would she do if he were to be killed? How could she bear it?

'Joyce, my dear,' he pleaded with her. 'You know how short we are of drivers. So many of the men have been called up. So I must do what I can. What would you want me to do? Let your father down?'

Joyce sighed. Yes, she knew that most of the able-bodied men who worked for her father had gone off to the war. At least she could take some comfort from the fact that George, because of his Argentinian citizenship, was still exempt.

'He's a God-send,' her father had said. He had warmed to George much more since the terrible bombing attacks on homes and families when George had been so valuable. 'A God-send.'

And that was the truth. Warmth stirred within Joyce, and pride. George was indeed a God-send, and not just to the business. Her eyes glowed. He had been heaven-sent... to her. And he made her world wonderful. That he kept the garage afloat virtually single-handedly, working so hard, doing so many hires... She was so proud of him.

She smiled fondly. 'Yes, of course. I know. It's just...' She blushed. Now he smiled in reply.

'I know. I was looking forward to our evening very much too...'

His eyes had such depths of velvety darkness, Joyce thought as she gazed into them. How she longed...

He bent and placed a tiny kiss on her temple, picked up his chauffeur's cap and turned to go. Joyce swallowed hard. He was so beautiful. Yes, beautiful was the only word for this man with his dark eyes and thick gleaming black hair, his tanned skin...

He paused and turned back.

'Unless...'

Joyce's heart leapt.

'Unless?' she echoed, fresh hope suddenly alive in her heart.

'Well, what I have to do on Friday evening is take the band's instruments out to the Christmas dance at Dunbeath,' George explained. He grinned. 'There might just be room for you, if you were willing to squeeze in the back with the drums...'

Joyce's face lit up. She would have agreed to anything for the chance of an evening with George.

'Yes,' she said. She laughed out loud with delight. 'I'd probably get my frock creased but that doesn't matter! I'm sure I can fit in beside the drums!'

CHAPTER 36

'See that she's home before midnight,' Joyce's father instructed George.

He had not been happy about this outing. George taking Joyce out in the car with him when it had been hired for another purpose seemed to Rab more than a little shabby.

'And I'm not too sure what kind of a crowd there will be at this dance,' he had confided to Joyce's mother.

'I must confess I'm still not too sure about *him*,' she had replied, 'but he makes Joyce happy and I'm grateful for that. She misses her big brother so much. She needs someone…'

Rab squeezed his wife's hand in gentle sympathy.

'Oh well,' Rab said. 'He's not a bad lad. We'll let her have her evening out. It is nearly Christmas after all.'

And so off they had gone. Joyce had squeezed cheerfully into the back of the big car beside the piano accordions and the drums. Her heart was dizzy with excitement, and her only worry was whether her frock would get irrevocably creased before they arrived at the dance.

She had been to country dances before but this one seemed more exciting, somehow more dangerous… Everyone seemed to be having a wonderful time. The band played the latest tunes as well as lots of old favourites. Most of the men were in uniform, mainly RAF and from other air forces – New Zealanders, Canadians, Polish. So many nationalities all intent on having a good night out. Despite the rationing, most of the girls looked lovely in colourful and pretty dresses, eyes bright with laughter and delight.

George brought her a drink. A real one. Wick was still dry, a temperance town where alcohol could only be got legally in the hotels or on the air base, but Dunbeath had not voted for prohibition, and the whisky, beer and other drinks flowed freely.

'Cheers!' he said, his eyes holding hers as she gingerly lifted the glass to her lips. He said it was apple juice but it had a bit of a kick. She liked it better by the second glass.

'This is fun!' she said, waving the glass at him. And it seemed as if the evening was even more fun as it went on – the colours brighter, the laughter louder, the crowd that packed into the hall friendlier.

And as the band began to play slower tunes and George drew her into his arms for a slow dance, Joyce rested her head on his shoulder and simply savoured the whole experience from a haze of wonder.

Is this really me? she thought as she felt his lips on her neck. *Is this me out dancing with this wonderful man?*

'Are you having fun?' his deliciously foreign voice enquired softly.

'Oh yes,' she breathed, snuggling closer to him.

'That's a pity,' he teased.

Joyce pulled away a little to study his face.

'Why?' she asked doubtfully.

'Because, *mi cariño*' – and here he disengaged his left arm from around her waist and showed her his watch – 'because it is time to take you home, or your papa will have me arrested, and I'll lose my job, and tomorrow morning I will be penniless and homeless and

133

probably in prison! And then you will have to come to visit me there and bring me food parcels...'

Joyce laughed. 'Silly!' she said.

'Seriously though,' George said. 'It is time to go.'

Joyce pouted, but George just laughed and dropped a butterfly kiss on her lips.

'Come on,' he said, and taking her hand led her to where she had left her coat.

She stumbled slightly as they walked from the hall towards where George had left the big black car. In the darkness she could hear rustlings and whispers, low voices and high giggles. Sudden bright spots showed a lit cigarette. It all felt deliciously naughty and she clung to George in delight, feeling him smile down at her, his dark eyes smouldering.

Unwilling to disengage from his encircling arm when they reached the car, Joyce turned into his embrace and lifted her face for his kiss. He pressed her back against the car and plundered her mouth. Breathless, she felt bereft when he pulled away and opened the car door. The back door.

'Your car awaits, my lady,' he said teasingly.

'But I want to sit with you,' Joyce said petulantly.

He pushed her into the back seat.

'And you will,' he said, as he followed in behind and gathered her to him.

CHAPTER 37

'Pregnant?' Ruby was shrill. 'How did that happen?'

She walked back through from the kitchen where she had been making a cup of tea and confronted George. He was relaxed in one of her mother's armchairs, legs stretched out in front of him.

'The usual way,' he said blandly.

Ruby glared at him. 'And what if *I* get pregnant again?' Ruby demanded. 'There's only one Cormack left to foist another child on and that won't work! Dan's fighting for home and country somewhere just a bit too far away for anyone to believe it this time.'

George drew on his cigarette and blew out a long stream of smoke in her face, forcing her to turn away.

'Then you'll just have to make sure that does not happen.' The words were cold and threatening.

Ruby stared at him. 'But...'

'There are no buts.' He fixed her with his eyes, hard and implacable. 'We are doing this my way. According to my plan. It's not my fault that your part of it did not work out.'

He held her eyes till she turned away. He waited calmly while she crashed crockery together in the kitchen and then returned with two cups of tea on a tray.

He took his cup and set it on the table next to him.

'Now that the late lamented Bobby will no longer inherit the garage, I simply have to make sure it falls directly into my hands. And the way to do that is via Joyce,' he explained patiently. 'A baby on the way effectively ensures that Joyce and the business will indeed fall into my hands. Her family would not wish for any scandal. We will be married and all will go as planned.'

'But what about me?' Ruby protested. 'Where do I come into all this? What am I going to do?'

'So long as you play your cards right, the Cormacks will look after you. After all, you are Bobby's widow and mother of his child.'

Ruby snorted.

'And if that's not enough for you, you could find yourself another unobservant husband, preferably a rich one,' George said with a mirthless grin. 'I'm sure you can.'

Ruby's answering smile was equally without mirth. 'That's a fact.' She paused. 'But I don't want another man.'

The silence built uncomfortably. She reached her hand out to George.

'I want only you.'

He took a last draw from his cigarette, then ground it hard into the ashtray on the table beside him.

'You know, Ruby my dear,' George said smoothly, 'that we cannot always have what we want or when we want it. Rest assured: our time will come. But for now, we need to do what we have to do. It's the only way to get what we really want. Let's not mess it up now.'

But as George finally left, he paused momentarily at the door, chauffeur's cap in hand, looking back at Ruby. She had appeared to accept his assurances but he would have to be careful. He could not afford for Ruby to spoil his plans.

He considered briefly, but he did not want to give her up, even temporarily. Of all the women he had known, Ruby was the only one he had ever involved in his plans, the only one he had worked *with*. She was his match in so many ways, his partner. But his plans had almost come undone with Bobby's death. He could take no further risks.

He would have to create some distance. Quickly he pulled his wallet out of his inside pocket and withdrew some notes, setting them on the mantelpiece. Ruby's eyes flashed as she watched him. Any other woman would have torn into him for the insult, but Ruby said nothing. Instead she rose and pocketed the money. George watched appreciatively. Her eyes told him she understood what he was saying. And the flounce in her step as she took the tea tray back to the kitchen, completely ignoring his departure, told him she remained undefeated.

He hid a smile. Ruby probably considered the money fairly earned. And it had been, in so many ways. It was a pity that he probably should not see her for a while, but it was for the best. The money would tide her over and give him a space to consolidate his position with the Cormacks.

As he walked downstairs and out to where he had left the car, he considered what needed to be done next. He had faced down Joyce's parents' anger. Stood by her side while she wept. Waited it out.

Her father's plain and honest anger was easy enough to deal with. Her mother... Now that was different. Those grey eyes seemed to search and see right down into his soul. If he had one.

He tried to shrug it off as he started the engine and drove the big black car out onto the road. Joyce's mother had looked at him – just looked – but it had felt like the most searching interrogation. And he felt sure he had been found wanting.

Then she had turned to Joyce and asked, very simply, 'My dear, is this what you want?'

For a moment, everything had teetered in the balance as he waited for Joyce to answer. One wrong word would destroy all his carefully laid plans. In that instant as he thought of all the hours he had spent working for her father, making himself indispensable, all the trouble he had taken to woo and seduce Joyce...

He had thought he had won over her mother too, but one glance at those implacable grey eyes told him he had been wrong. Could he have been wrong about Joyce too?

But no. She looked up at him, eyes bright with tears, cheeks reddened with the shame of her situation, but her lips curved in trembling joy. She tugged at his hand holding hers.

'Yes!' she declared with defiant joy. 'Yes, of course it's what I want. We love each other and everything will be all right!'

And she had plastered herself up against him, expecting his enthusiastic response. Which, with her parents watching, he had to provide. Especially with her mother watching, with those searching grey eyes.

So he had embraced Joyce and kissed her, kissed the tears on her cheeks and protested in carefully broken English his sorrow that it had come to this. That he had wanted better for her...

And as he had expected, she had assured him that it was all right. That it would be all right.

And so they were to be married.

As the car purred back towards Wick, George had to admit that he had handled it all rather well.

CHAPTER 38

Manitoba, Canada, 1941

They laid Katie to rest in the little churchyard in town close to where Bill and Marie and Clem were buried. Afterwards friends and family gathered at the ranch house where Nancy and Katie's mother welcomed them and plied them with refreshments. Despite the warmth of the goodwill and a generous spread of food, it was a sombre occasion with Hugh barely able to speak to the kind folks who had come to offer their condolences.

Nancy watched him, concern in her eyes. He shook hands, accepted the kindly words, but she could tell he was armoured against them, his eyes dull. The only exception was when Hugo got away from the young cousin who was supposed to be looking after him and came to Hugh's side.

Hugh bent and put his hand on the boy's shoulder, sudden tears in his eyes. He murmured something to him, then he held him close for a moment till Hugo grew restless and took himself off again. After that, Hugh's eyes never left Hugo, his last link with Katie.

When at last everyone had gone and the helpers had cleared everything away, Nancy went to find him. They had stood waving their goodbyes on the porch and Nancy had then gone to supervise the clear-up. But when at last all was done, there was no sign of Hugh.

She found him in Hugo's bedroom, standing silently gazing at the sleeping youngster in the small bed.

Nancy reached up to put her hand on his arm. Hugh turned and she saw the tears in his eyes.

'He's all I've got,' Hugh said. 'He's all that matters now.'

'And you'll look after him and bring him up well,' Nancy said. 'I know you will.'

A brief smile flickered across Hugh's face. 'Well, I had a good example, didn't I?'

Nancy leaned up on her toes and kissed his cheek.

'Thank you,' she said.

'Thank *you*,' Hugh corrected her. 'You taught me what was important. You *showed* me what was important, you and Clem.' He sighed. 'I wanted what you had, you and Clem, and what Bill and Marie had – a long and happy marriage.' He swallowed hard. 'But it wasn't to be.'

And then suddenly he was in her arms, the big strong rancher once more the hurting little boy she had comforted so often.

'Oh Mama, how am I to go on without her?' Hugh murmured brokenly. 'She was my whole world! I loved her so much!'

Nancy stroked his hair as she chose her words carefully. 'Maybe there's something else you can learn from me and Clem.'

Hugh straightened and focused to listen to her.

'Love never dies,' Nancy said quietly. 'That's what I've learned.'

Hugh gazed at her, questioning.

'If it's real love – like Clem and I had, like I believe you and Katie had – then nothing can take it away. It stays, inside you. Keeps you warm when you're cold and gives you something to hang on to when you're lonely.'

She smiled at his sudden surprised reaction.

'Yes, I often get sad and lonely. I miss Clem terribly. And that never goes away. I know he's gone to be with the Lord, and that we'll meet again one day. Just as you know you will with Katie. You both trusted the Lord.'

Hugh nodded.

Marie continued softly so as not to waken the sleeping child. 'People say time heals. It doesn't. A loss is a loss is a loss, and the pain will always be there. Some days it's less; other days it leaps up and hurts you all over again. The trick to staying human is to accept that pain. Keep your heart open and let it through. If you try to shut it out in any way – and there are lots of ways the world offers! Some men hit the bottle; others throw themselves into the first pair of willing arms...'

She was glad to note Hugh's instinctive revulsion.

'Well, it's a common temptation,' she said. 'And if you fell for it, all you'd be doing would be putting a plaster on a wound that needs the air. When the plaster falls off or rots off, as it inevitably does, the pain will simply come back with fresh power. And it will have made a mess of what would otherwise have been clean healing.'

She patted his arm. 'So it's good that you grieve. It shows that you loved Katie. It's good that you value Hugo and don't turn from him. He needs you – but you need him too...'

Again Hugh stared at her questioningly.

'You need a safe place for your love now that Katie's gone,' Nancy explained, 'and loving Hugo is safe. Till you heal. And that will take time.'

They turned back to the bed as the young lad moved and murmured suddenly in his sleep.

'Kiss him goodnight,' Nancy instructed Hugh.

Her eyes twinkled as he bent to obey. He had always been an obedient son. But her face was sombre again as she considered how much he would need her in the days to come. And she was not getting any younger.

CHAPTER 39

Wick, 1941

'She needs her mother.' Those grey eyes fixed steadily on George. 'Especially at a time like this.'

George had to admit it was easier to have Joyce's mother cope with her morning sickness and her emotional ups and downs than have to deal with them himself. In the days and weeks leading up to their marriage, the town had suffered more enemy attacks, shredding Joyce's nerves to ribbons, and her pregnancy seemed to make her even more emotional.

One surprising benefit of the October attack on Hill Avenue the previous year was the damage to the nearby Bignold Hospital. The blast had rocked the building, dislodging swathes of plaster and making it unfit for use. Casualties needing treatment now had to be taken to Lybster, where the big new school had been requisitioned for use as a hospital and all the staff transferred. And Lybster was not only the most convenient pick-up point for illicit alcohol in the area, but was also where Ruby was still living with her mother. Instead of having to limit his visits to Ruby, he could now easily combine business *and* pleasure, so long as he was careful.

This convenience pleased George as he made the frequent trips out to the hospital with patients in the ambulance, and visitors, family and friends in one of the cars. There was no need to make up stories or excuses. While Joyce was still able to work in the office, she could see exactly where he was going and why.

And so he was able to accept with apparently good grace the irritations of living with the Cormacks in the house adjoining the office and garage in Francis Street after he and Joyce married. Let her mother continue to mother her. It freed him up to live his life as he chose. All he needed to do was play the devoted husband when in the company of the Cormacks and continue to be indispensable to the business.

'So charming,' the ladies of the town enthused.

'So very helpful,' as he fetched and carried for them with his trademark smile.

'Like a film star!'

'Quite an asset,' he heard Joyce's mother's quiet response to a visiting cousin.

'And Joyce?'

'She is well and happy.' Again spoken quietly and determinedly.

George wondered just what Hannah Cormack really thought of her daughter's choice. It was clear, though, that she kept a watchful eye on him. Coming from a large local family, she had innumerable cousins and connections – so many it sometimes seemed she had eyes everywhere. He knew he had to be careful... for a while yet.

But when Joyce gave birth, in early September 1941, he could not quite keep back his appalled disappointment. He wanted a son! He *needed* a son! To consolidate his position and have an heir to inherit the garage, he needed a son! And the stupid useless woman had given him a daughter!

He slammed out of the house and stormed through the streets till he found a place where he knew he would get a much-needed drink.

The door was quickly opened and a tumbler of whisky set in front of him. He downed it in one.

'Wetting the baby's head?' a wit enquired.

George glared at the man, eyes mad with fury. The owner of the shebeen brought the bottle and set it on the table. George accepted with a nod and poured out a generous shot. As he swallowed the fiery liquor down, he remembered the first time he had come here – with Ruby. How many years ago? And what had he to show for it? Two daughters! By two useless women! And a job! Honest employment! Him!

What had happened to his planned future? Once he had hoped for an inheritance here – a castle or two, land, wealth. When he discovered that was a fairytale, he had decided to put to good use his Chicago experience running illegal whisky. To do that he needed transport – and so he had gone to work for Rab Cormack. And that had given him another idea and he had plotted and schemed and manoeuvred and manipulated – and where had it got him?

The future stretched ahead of him like a prison sentence – straight and narrow. Marriage to the oh-so-respectable Joyce. Being the loving husband and indispensable son-in-law to her sharp-eyed mother and penny-pinching father. Stuck here in this cold grey town for the rest of his life. He wasn't forty yet! There had to be more to life!

'Well, hello! Fancy seeing you here!'

Ruby slid into the chair next to him. She gestured to the whisky bottle and his empty tumbler.

'Celebrating? Or drowning your sorrows?'

'Just having a drink,' he said.

Her eyes narrowed. 'Has Joyce had the baby? Is that it?' She watched as George swallowed another slug of whisky.

'Ah,' she said, sitting back, a catlike grin on her face. 'Don't tell me. Another girl?' She searched his face. 'I'm right, aren't I? Not the son and heir you wanted.'

He slammed the empty tumbler down on the table. 'None of your business.'

'Oh I don't know,' Ruby said thoughtfully. 'A sister for Amanda. What is she going to be called?'

'Georgina.'

'That's nice,' Ruby said blithely. 'After her dad. Quite usual in these parts to give family names...'

But George ignored her, staring grimly into his glass.

'Of course some family names are not so popular...' Ruby continued, unconcerned by his lack of response. 'There's one name you could choose for her that would really annoy the Cormacks.'

George looked up, his interest suddenly piqued. 'What's that?'

'Belle,' Ruby announced.

'What's wrong with Belle?' George asked. 'Perfectly normal name.'

'Not for that family,' Ruby said with a knowing smile. 'Belle was Rab Cormack's first wife. Bobby's mother. Not that he ever knew her. She died in childbirth...'

'And?' George demanded.

'And seemingly that was a blessing in disguise,' Ruby said. 'She was the black sheep of the family. There was quite a lot of scandal that they don't like being reminded about. But of course you'd have to pretend you didn't know...' She grinned mischievously.

George topped up their glasses.

'I like the sound of this,' he said. 'Tell me all about Belle.'

CHAPTER 40

Manitoba, 1942

Hugh stood bareheaded in the cold Canadian afternoon. Hat in hand, he was barely aware of the people around him, as the minister said prayers over the coffin that had just been gently laid to rest in the open grave. He hated this cemetery. He had avoided it like the plague in the aftermath of Katie's death, but the dead man was an old friend and Hugh felt he had no choice but to force himself to attend the ceremony.

He gazed bleakly around him. Despite being surrounded by the crowd of folk who had turned out for this funeral, Hugh felt very alone. So many of the people he had loved most in the world were buried in this small graveyard. His beloved Grandpa Bill and Mama Marie. His wise and loving stepfather Clem. And his darling Katie.

Hugh raised his eyes to the hills that circled the peaceful cemetery and the words of an old psalm came back to him: '*I will lift up mine eyes unto the hills, from whence cometh my help.*'[1]*

---

1 * Psalm 121

He remembered Mama Marie patiently explaining to him that the comma in the middle was a mistake. That it should really be a full stop. The text should go, she said, '*I will lift up mine eyes unto the hills. From whence cometh my help?*' And then the answer was in the next line: '*My help cometh from the* LORD.'

At the time, it had made sense. He had accepted everything his family had taught him about the God they believed in. But he was very young then and untouched by life. Now he knew things were not so simple.

Hugh managed by sheer force of will to stop the angry scowl settling back on his face, but the words of the psalm rolled round in his head, challenging him. Help? From the Lord? From the very One who instead of helping, had taken away the people he loved? The people he needed? The one special person he still desperately needed.

He stared at the hills. Might as well as leave the comma in, he told Marie in the dark aching silence of his heart. I get as much help from those unmoving lumps of rock as I do from your God.

He shifted restlessly as the graveside ceremony drew to a close. He needed help. From somewhere. But where? What was he going to do?

After Katie's death, his mother had remained to look after him and Hugo. She had done her best but, as she said herself, she was not getting any younger. That was why, with her agreement, Hugh had brought in a girl from the town – someone they knew from church – to help her. Unfortunately the girl had thought this might be the stepping stone to a different role at the ranch – one where she was mistress instead of simply a hired hand – and she had had to be let go.

But something needed to be done. Nancy really was not able to go on carrying all the work. She needed to be back in her little house in town among her friends, looking after her own needs. What he needed, Hugh knew, was a sensible person to be their housekeeper.

Finally the service was over. As he left the graveside, a rustle of skirts almost in his path made Hugh slow and look up. It was the girl he had sent away. The girl with ideas.

He eyed her with disfavour, but she saw him looking at her and sent him a speaking glance. Oh dear. It seemed she was still willing.

Briefly, coldly, he considered his options. He could do worse. His mother could work herself into an early grave and he did not want that. He could not face another funeral in this bleak little graveyard. Maybe if he went into it with his eyes open, expecting no more than a clean house, a hot meal and a warm bed, maybe it would not be so much a mistake as a sensible transaction?

There would never be anyone to match his Katie. No one could ever replace her, so there was no point trying. But he had to be sensible. They could not go on as they were.

There was a delay as he queued to shake hands and offer condolences to the family, then he sought out the girl and almost despairingly spoke to her. And it was agreed.

So finally he could go home to the ranch, but Hugo was waiting for him, full of his news as only a ten-year-old can be.

Hugh tried to show interest in all the lad's adventures but his heart was not in it. So he broke the news to him, as simply and as pragmatically as he could.

Hugo at once protested. 'But we can manage! We don't need anyone, and anyway...'

Hugh frowned. 'And anyway what?'

But Hugo simply shrugged. 'What do I know?' he said and took himself out, but his shoulders were slumped in misery.

'I'm doing this for you!' Hugh wanted to shout after him.

But that was not entirely true. He needed – wanted – a woman about the house, and if the only way to get one was to marry one, then he was willing to do that.

And he was willing. Willing to let the girl have her special day, dressed in all her finery, and stars in her silly eyes.

~

Once more, Hugh found himself at the little church in town accepting handshakes from the church folks. All the church families declared themselves delighted. An excellent match. A mother for Hugo. Nancy, Hugh noticed, said little.

He took the girl by the hand and led her out to the buggy. His new wife. She waved and threw her bouquet of flowers to her waiting, cheering friends.

'See you on Sunday!' she called as they drove off.

Hugh was silent, then he said, 'You go by all means. I'll make sure there's a driver for the buggy.'

'But what about you?' She turned to him in surprise. 'Surely we go to church together!'

Hugh shook his head as he whipped up the team. 'No,' he said quietly. 'If you want to go, you go. I might find time at Christmas and Easter. But I don't see it's ever done me any good so I don't think I'll waste any more of my time on it.'

Her mouth thinned but she did not challenge him.

Good, Hugh thought. She needed to know right from the outset who was boss.

CHAPTER 41

Wick

'Oh, George! This is wonderful!'

Joyce's eyes shone as she gazed around the sitting room of the little house he had found for them. Eagerly she scurried through to the kitchen and then upstairs to check out the bedrooms.

As George waited for her downstairs, he thought back to his Grandpapa de la Vega's fine villa in one of the smartest districts of Buenos Aires. He recalled his stepfather Ramon's gracious hacienda out in the pampas, centre of his ranching empire. And there was Al Capone's house in Chicago where George had so often swept up to the door in the limousine to carry Mary Capone to her weekly appointment at the hairdresser's.

This little grey stone two-up two-down terraced cottage in a cold windswept coastal town in Caithness in no way stood in the same rank. But when he had told Joyce he had found them a home, it instantly achieved what was required. It had pleased Joyce. More to the point, it had pleased Joyce's parents, especially Joyce's father.

'Well done,' Rab Cormack had said approvingly. 'It will be good for Joyce to have her own home now the baby has arrived. Her mother loved having her at home here with us, but you're a family now, and a family needs their own house.'

So now they would settle into boring family life in the little house in Kinnaird Street. George consoled himself that at least he would be out from under the sharp grey eyes of Joyce's mother. Joyce seemed in seventh heaven and she sang George's praises to her parents at every opportunity. And gradually Papa Cormack was beginning to loosen the reins of the business.

The shock of Bobby's death had taken its toll and Rab seemed grateful to George for stepping into the breach. The old man had aged visibly in the past year. Although he claimed to be in perfect health, George was sure he was not. He had seen the blue lips and the white knuckles as the old man steadied himself after strenuous work in the garage. His heart was surely wearing out.

It could not come soon enough for George. Those bottles of whisky tucked securely into the upholstery of the back seat where he had seduced Joyce after the dance in Dunbeath had grown into a lucrative business. Just as in Prohibition Chicago, making alcohol illegal had simply made it more desirable – and the respectable burghers of Wick who were unwilling or unable to travel for their pleasures were more than willing to pay a little extra for home deliveries. Keeping Ruby involved in the business had been a sound move too. She continued to arrange for the whisky to be delivered to her mother's house, and he was able to pick up the consignments when he visited her. The geographical separation of the two sides of his life made them both operate perfectly.

And as word got round in the local small-time underworld that George was the man with transport who was able to help and willing to turn a blind eye, it became clear that he had found his niche. Drawing on his experiences in Chicago, he found more and more imaginative ways to transport and deliver the illegal beverages. There were plenty of places to stash a bottle in an ambulance, and even the hearse offered facilities which were most welcome to men returning from a chilly graveside on a cold day.

And there was good money in it. Enough to keep both Joyce and Ruby satisfied. And some over to fund George's increasingly enjoyable gambling activities.

George smiled as he watched Joyce survey her new domain. Having their own house would give him much more freedom. Living in the Francis Street house with her parents had been bad enough, but always being on call for work and his every movement having to be accounted for had been intolerable.

Yet the Cormacks took it for granted.

'Building a business takes sacrifice,' Mr Cormack said, as if it was something worthy of pride.

And his wife had smiled, saying, 'But now maybe it's our time to slow down. Leave you young ones to do the hard work!'

George had suppressed his impatience. The handover of the business could not come soon enough for him. If he had his way, Mr Cormack would work himself into a sudden apoplexy and die amidst the streaks of oil on the garage floor, leaving the way clear for him rather than remaining a constant watchful presence, on the sidelines.

Patience, George counselled himself. As he had planned, Mr Cormack had released much of the management of the business and nearly all of the work to him. It was simply a pity that his father-in-law still retained control of the purse strings. It was surely only a matter of time before Rab Cormack's heart gave out...

If only Joyce would produce that son and heir for the business – then Mr Cormack could be brought to see he could safely hand it all over and retire. Another baby. That surely was the answer.

But there was one other worry nagging at George. Prohibition had only lasted around thirteen years in Chicago before it was repealed. The town of Wick had voted to be dry in 1922, but the move to bring back alcohol was vocal and growing. Should that happen, George knew his whole profitable illegal enterprise would disappear overnight.

He had to secure some kind of future.

CHAPTER 42

'Do you really have to go out?' Joyce asked plaintively.

It had been a long hard day. Rab Cormack had been on his case all day long and when George got home, the baby had been crying, the fire smoking unpleasantly, and his dinner unappetising. He looked now at the complaining face in front of him and his patience snapped. He did not need this. He needed a quiet drink.

'Yes,' he growled, picking up his chauffeur's cap from the sideboard and making for the door.

'Dada!'

The infant on the floor reached out to him suddenly and as George tried to avoid her sticky clutching hands, he stepped on a discarded building block and lost his balance. As he crashed into the dining table, the edge cutting into his side, a torrent of Spanish exploded from his lips – words he had not used in years.

Though Joyce knew no Spanish, it was clear from the sound what kind of words they were.

'George!' she protested, covering her hands with her ears.

Painfully he levered himself off the table and turned. There she stood, his wife these last two years. She had put on weight and her now lumpy figure was unattractively tied into a stained apron. Her face was pasty, her hair unkempt.

Joyce withered before his critical gaze and bent to pick up the child, holding her in her arms protectively like a shield before her.

But something in the torrent of Spanish had unlocked something deep inside George. Reminding him of the man he used to be. Before he got caught up in – this.

A knife twisted. He looked at the woman and child calculatingly.

'Put the child down,' he instructed.

Joyce hesitated.

In an instant he was at her side and had struck her across the face.

'Oh!' she cried in surprise and pain.

His eyes bored into her.

'I said: put the child down. Do I have to repeat myself?' He held his hand up. 'Am I not master in my own house?'

Fearfully she put the child down on the floor.

'George,' she pleaded, swallowing hard, fear in her eyes.

'Better,' he said. Then stepped in and struck her again, hard. 'But you will obey me faster next time.'

And he turned and sauntered out, leaving Joyce staring after him in disbelief.

CHAPTER 43

Manitoba, 1943

Hugh flung himself onto his horse and turned its head towards the trail. He had to get away.

What was it about women? They were nothing but trouble. Hugh's angry thoughts burned inside him. He kicked into his horse's sides and set himself to outride his demons. The chill air and the wide-open spaces welcomed him, offering peace, freedom…

But she would still be there when he got back. That was the worst of it. How was he ever going to get free? It had all been the most terrible mistake. He should never have married her.

Worse, she was making Hugo's life a misery. Complaining, criticising, nagging, and never letting up from sun-up till sun-down.

And Hugo's peaceful nature was changing. Hugh had heard the odd snap, the young voice suddenly sharp.

But she had snapped back, 'Don't you speak to me like that. I'll tell your father.'

And Hugo's response had been weary and apathetic: 'Tell all you like. I don't care.'

Where was the boy? Hugh realised he had not seen him all day. He slowed his horse's pace. Maybe he should go and look for him. Spend some time with him. Just peaceful father-and-son time.

It had been a long time since they had done that.

As he turned the horse round to return to the ranch buildings, Hugh thought about that. It had not really been so long. It just felt like that. Every day felt like a weary lifetime now, a prison sentence that would never end. And as he saw the future stretching out ahead of him – with the bad-tempered never-satisfied shrew he had left in the ranch house – he knew he had to do something. But what?

Mama Marie – she had been born and raised a Catholic. For him to be even contemplating divorce would be horrifying to her. His own mother, quietly settled in the township where her beloved Clem had pastored for so many years – it would bring shame and disgrace to her door. People like them did not divorce.

But, Hugh thought wearily, people like them maybe did not rush into stupid relationships and thereby get themselves trapped in misery. For himself, he could probably find a way to endure. But Hugo was being hurt and that, he would not permit.

Quietly he rode the horse back to the barn and tethered it at the rail outside.

'Seen Hugo?' he asked one of the lads, but there was only a shake of the head.

Hugh strolled round the buildings, looking for Hugo, but as the afternoon wore on, he began to feel anxious. No one seemed to know where the lad was. When he asked when he had last been seen, he was greeted by shrugs.

He began to wonder whether they all knew exactly where Hugo was but were deliberately not letting on. That they were protecting him. But why? He and Hugo had not fallen out. Hugo had no need to hide from him. Hugo was popular with the ranch hands, but Hugh hoped he was a fair boss. Surely they would not hide things from him?

At last, his worry drove him to the bunkhouse where he knew he would find someone who would tell him what was going on. As he expected, old Albert was ensconced comfortably in his armchair, dozing by the fire. The old man had worked for Papa Bill for many long years and Hugh had been glad of his wisdom and guiding hand after Bill died and the reins of the ranch came into his hands.

When the old man was no longer able to work the cattle or the horses, Hugh had insisted his home would always be the ranch. He had ensured that there was not only a comfortable place for Albert in the bunkhouse but everything he needed. Hugh had got in the habit of dropping in for a long chat with Albert – and chewing over anything he needed help with. But, Hugh realised, he had not visited Albert for a while.

The sound of the door closing woke Albert from his doze and his eyes fixed on Hugh. To his surprise, Albert's face filled with fright at the sight of him.

'No! No! Please, no!'

He clutched the blanket that covered his knees as if afraid it would be torn from him.

'Albert!' Hugh said, going close, but Albert raised a hand as if to ward him away.

'Please, do not say it! Do not do this!' Albert pleaded in a thin reedy voice. 'I am no trouble, I promise you. I eat very little. I…'

'What is this?' Hugh demanded. 'What are you worrying about?'

'Please do not send me away!' Albert said and there were tears in his old eyes. 'This is my home. You are my people…'

Hugh put his hand on Albert's and tried to soothe him. 'Old friend, I would not send you away. This is your home for as long as you wish it, as long as you need it.'

But the old man was shaking his head and rocking in distress.

Hugh knelt down so he could look straight into Albert's face.

'Albert, no one is saying anything about sending you away!'

But Albert continued to shake his head in great distress.

Hugh sat back on his heels and took the old man's hands in a strong grip.

'Albert, I assure you – I give you my word – that I would never send you away...'

'Not of your own free will!' came the sad reply.

'What do you mean?' Hugh asked, baffled. 'I decide what happens on this ranch...'

But Albert gave a miserable snicker and shook his head.

'Not now,' he said with a sigh. 'Not any more.'

Hugh stared at the old man. What could he mean? And then the penny dropped. He could not even call his life his own...

But that was different. That was marriage. With Katie he delighted to share his life, to pour it out at her feet. He had done everything for her willingly. The pain of her loss kicked in again, fresh and new. How he missed her! How could he ever have thought he could replace her with this... poor pretend substitute.

There. It was said. And no, he could not call his life his own but it was no longer a thing of joy. It was miserable servitude.

'Tell me,' Hugh said softly, crouching closer beside Albert's chair. 'Tell me what she said, what she has done.'

And Albert poured out his story to Hugh.

'*I am the mistress here,*' Albert mimicked softly. '*And we don't need useless old men like you cluttering up the place...*'

160

'Did she now?' Hugh asked slowly.

Albert nodded, tears rolling down his thin cheeks.

Hugh rose and patted his shoulder. 'As far as I know, I am still the boss here,' he said. 'And you're going nowhere – unless you want to!'

Albert shook his head decisively.

'Then that's settled,' Hugh said. He turned to leave, then recalled why he had come to see Albert. 'By the way,' he asked, 'you don't happen to have seen Hugo, have you?'

He was surprised by the flash of anger that crossed Albert's face.

'What's the matter? Has Hugo done something…'

'Not him,' Albert said. '*Her.*'

Hugh drew in a calming breath. 'Tell me.'

'She said he was an unmanageable no-good and if he didn't sort himself out, she would see to it that he was sent away to school. And that she'd get you to disinherit him so he could never come back to the ranch…'

But Hugh barely heard the last words. Fuelled by fury, he was on his way across the yard to the ranch house.

CHAPTER 44

She was in the kitchen, folding laundry, thumping each piece crossly into the basket, her back towards him. Hugh watched her for a few moments while he strove to regain his temper. But when she turned and gave that superior tight smile, saying, 'And now what's the problem?' he nearly bundled her in the laundry and sent her on her way there and then.

But he knew that was not the way to deal with this.

'Problem?' he echoed, carefully controlling his voice. 'Should there be a problem?'

Her eyes narrowed.

'Then what are you doing here?' she snapped. 'You must want something.'

Hugh raised an eyebrow. 'I think maybe I can go wherever I like on my own land,' he said quietly.

Her mouth opened to retort but he spoke first. 'And do pretty much whatever I like on my own ranch.'

Nettled, her mouth clamped down on whatever it was she had been going to say. Knowing it would annoy her, Hugh went over to the cookie jar and helped himself to a cookie. He watched her anger rising as he raised it to his mouth.

'I think I paid for these,' he forestalled her. 'So I think I'm entitled to eat them.'

'And I baked them,' she snapped.

'So you did,' he agreed and helped himself to a second cookie. 'By the way, do you happen to know where that...' He paused, then added carefully: '...unmanageable no-good son of mine is?' He watched the ugly red flush rise in her cheeks.

'No business of mine,' she said, turning away.

'No? And I had hoped you would be a loving mother to him.' Hugh waited but there was no reaction. 'And what about old Albert? I hope you've been looking after him?'

'Oh, is that what this is all about?' she demanded, turning back with fire in her eyes. 'That useless old man. Someone needed to say it. You just let everyone ride roughshod over you. The place would go to rack and ruin if I didn't...'

'Mmm,' Hugh said thoughtfully. 'I rather thought the place had been doing fine when it was just me and the boys and old Albert here. And I rather thought the only person who has been doing any riding roughshod over any of us – me, the boy, old Albert to name a few...' Hugh paused, watching her face: '...has been you.'

She gasped. 'How dare you! I'm your wife! All I've been trying to do is help you!'

'By driving my boy away? By reducing an old man who never did anyone any harm but did me and my family only good through the years – reducing him to tears of fear that he's about to be thrown out of the only home he has ever known? And as for me...'

'As for you! You only get what you deserve!' she threw at him. 'I don't know why I ever agreed to marry you! All you wanted was a replacement to do the woman's work around here – in your kitchen, with your son, in your bed! Well, I'm sick of it. It's been a bad bargain but I've done my best and if you're not satisfied...'

The answer was clear in his eyes. She faltered to a stop.

Hugh folded his arms. 'You're right. It was a bad bargain. For us both. And no, I'm not satisfied.' He waited but she said nothing. 'And if you're honest with yourself, you're not satisfied either.' He smiled wearily. 'I reckon you can do better than this. And if you'll help me sort this out peaceably, I'll help you in whatever way you want.'

He could see the sudden calculation in her eyes.

'Whatever way?' she echoed.

'If it's possible and legal,' Hugh answered.

CHAPTER 45

'Were you very unhappy?' Hugh asked his son.

They sat by the creek surrounded by their fishing gear, idly waiting for the fish to bite. It had been a good day. The first, Hugh hoped, of many.

'Yes,' Hugo said quietly. 'But I could see it was worse for you. I thought if I went away maybe she'd stop using me in her fights with you...'

'I'm sorry, son,' Hugh said. 'It was all my fault. I should never have married her.'

A tug on a line and all their attention switched to the possible catch, but after a short tussle, the prey got away.

'Live to fight another day,' Hugh said.

'Like you, Dad,' Hugo said.

'Me?' He laughed. 'No, I'm older and wiser now! No more women.'

'She did have one good idea,' Hugo began tentatively.

'What's that?' Hugh asked.

'School.'

'What do you mean, "school"?'

'When she talked about you sending me away to school, at first I hated the idea, but the more I thought about it, I began to wonder. So I set about finding out what the possibilities might be, and the more I found out, the more I began to think it could be a good idea.' Hugo plucked at the grass on the bank beside him. 'I love the ranch,' he assured his father. 'But maybe it's not what I want to do with my life.'

Hugh raised an eyebrow in surprise. He had never thought further than Hugo inheriting the ranch once day, as he had, and running it, as he had.

'No? So what would you like to do?'

'I don't know. I'm interested in the business side of things…' Hugo said. 'I was thinking I'd like to study that. At university when I'm old enough. But I'd need the right qualifications, the right entrance exams.'

Hugh looked over at his son's earnest face. It had come alive with enthusiasm. So this was something Hugo cared about. That was good, though it would be a wrench to let him go. Hugh chose his words carefully.

'And maybe school somewhere would help?'

'Yep.'

Hugh thought about their situation. The break-up of his second marriage had left a bad taste he was struggling to overcome. He found it increasingly uncomfortable to go into town where the girl's family lived, though his mother had been pragmatic about it.

'You made a mistake, love,' she said. 'God forgives. Now you need to forgive yourself and get on with your life.' She had grinned at him suddenly. 'And maybe you won't make that mistake again!'

'Never!' he had declared, but she had put a finger on his lips.

'We're weak human beings, my love,' she said affectionately. 'Don't say never! Just be careful!'

He was determined about that. He had thrown himself back into the work of the ranch, trying to erase every trace of the toxic presence that had so spoiled things between him and Hugo. But it had not worked.

He discovered it was not possible to simply turn the clock back. And anyway, where could he turn it back to that he wanted to be? Katie would never be there again, and that was all he really wanted.

So it came as a kind of relief that Hugo was ready for a change of scene. Maybe it was time for a change for both of them.

Just the other day he had seen a newspaper article about the war in Europe. It appeared the Canadian government was trying to put together a new Forestry Corps to go to Britain to help the war effort there. Men with relevant experience were being invited to sign up. Age did not seem to matter.

Hugh had reread the piece with sudden longing. How he would like to just up and go. But there was Hugo. He needed to stay here at the ranch till Hugo was grown.

But Hugo was now suggesting he would like to go away to school. Boarding school. And if that could be arranged, then Hugh would be free to do... whatever he liked.

He thought of the article about the Forestry Corps. He had relevant experience. He turned suddenly hopeful eyes on Hugo.

'I reckon this idea of yours is a good one,' he began.

CHAPTER 46

Wick, 1943

'No, I'd love to. Truly, Mum,' Joyce said. 'It's just...' She racked her brains for an excuse her mother would accept without too many questions. 'Georgie's got a bit of a temperature and I don't want to take her out in the cold.'

As she put down the telephone, she caught sight of herself in the mirror on the wall above it. The telephone was really for George – for calls from the garage – but her mother occasionally rang and so long as George was out, Joyce felt safe to answer it. She stared into the mirror, into her own eyes – dark and blank with the horror of life as it was now. With George as he was now.

She saw the latest bruise on her cheek and she knew she could not let her mother see it. Make-up would not cover it, no matter how skilfully she tried to apply it. And she had never been that clever with make-up.

Tears began to roll down her cheeks, tears of helplessness. What was she to do?

'Mama,' the child in the next room called out to her. Joyce hurried to pacify her. She had learnt that George did not tolerate interruptions, even from his own child.

The list of things that George did not tolerate had grown and grown until she felt it would never be possible to please him. She lived in constant fear of something triggering his anger. She sometimes felt he came home looking for an excuse, something he could pick on as a reason for the next beating.

What had happened to him? Where had the delightful Prince Charming of her dreams gone?

Joyce sank into the armchair, Georgie in her arms. Bending her cheek to the little girl's soft dark hair, Joyce let the tears flow.

Her parents must never know. It would kill her father. His heart, already shaken by Bobby's death in the early years of the war, had taken a number of knocks as he tried to continue running the garage on a skeleton staff of men not liable to be called up – and George. He depended on George.

What would he do without George? If he knew how George had been treating her... George would be out of the garage and the town before he could draw breath.

Did she want that?

Joyce stilled. It was an impossible choice. For her father's sake, she knew she had to keep quiet.

The little one looked up and smiled at her. Dark eyes, dark hair like her father. A winsome, charming smile. Like her father.

Georgina Belle.

George had registered the names.

'I thought you'd be pleased,' he had said when she protested, aghast. 'Traditional family names. I thought you'd like that.'

But she had wondered. Surely he knew how much it would hurt her mother for her granddaughter to be named after the sister who had done her so much harm? At the time it had seemed an unlikely act of malice. Of cruelty. But now... Joyce's hand came

169

up involuntarily to the bruise on her face. Now, she was not so sure.

Joyce sighed. Had she ever been in love with George? Or had it been a silly young girl's fantasy? Humming softly as she rocked the child gently on her lap, Joyce thought back over the years from when George had appeared – so foreign and dashing, so exciting, and different. Was that what the attraction had been? That he was different? Exotic? And slightly dangerous too?

She had to admit there had always been an undercurrent of danger with George. Of threat, menace even. She shivered.

At first it had been exciting and she had felt so alive, so adventurous and grown-up. A sophisticated woman, going out with him. She knew Ruby fancied him and so it had added extra spice to flaunt her growing relationship with George. How foolish she had been! She dropped a kiss on the child's head.

She had been a star-struck child, with no more sense than this one. She smiled with a trace of bitterness. George had certainly made sure she grew up.

Gone were her starry eyes and blissful ideals of marriage and happy-ever-after. Now she was trapped in her own home, terrified of the sound of his step and the door opening. What kind of a mood would he be in? How bad a beating would she get this time?

It was no kind of a life. Joyce set the child to face her and gazed into her eyes.

'If it was you, and I was your mum…' she began slowly.

A soft tread behind her made her freeze in terror. She was not expecting George home so soon. She could not bear to look round.

'George,' she said in a voice shuddering with fear. 'George, I…'

But the hand on her shoulder was soft and warm and consoling.

'It's not George, my darling. It's me.'

Joyce turned in glowing relief, the tears filling her eyes, to face her mother. And in that instant her mother took in the bruise on Joyce's face, and Joyce saw the horror in her mother's eyes. She tried to hide the bruise, to wave her mother away. But her mother stood her ground, those steady grey eyes filled with sudden comprehension and a wealth of compassion.

'You were saying, my dear,' she said. 'If it was you, and I was your mum...'

Joyce nodded mutely.

'Were you going to say: what would I tell you to do?'

Joyce's eyes dropped. Again she laid her head against the soft dark hair of her young daughter, and the tears of hopelessness coursed from between her eyelids.

'I think you know what I'd tell you to do,' her mother said. 'I'd tell you to come home. You and the little one. Come home. We'll look after you.'

She gestured to the livid bruise on Joyce's cheek.

'And we'd protect you so *that* never happens again.'

CHAPTER 47

Hannah Cormack kissed her daughter's forehead. She set down her handbag and took off her coat.

'Will you let me have a look at that?' she asked.

Joyce shook her head, shame in her eyes.

'Do you have any other bruises?'

The question was gentle, but her mother was clearly determined to get an answer.

'Yes,' Joyce whispered, thinking of the livid patches on her arms and torso, green and purple, old and newer bruises. Her body had become a punchbag.

'My darling, whatever is going on I know you are not to blame.'

'Oh, but I am!' Joyce cried out. 'If I hadn't been so stupid as to get involved with George in the first place.' She blushed painfully. 'And to get pregnant!' Her eyes searched her mother's. 'I'm so sorry! I shamed you all! And now... Now this!' She gestured to the bruise on her cheek. 'Oh Mum! Things like this don't happen in our family! What am I going to do?'

Hannah carefully extricated Georgie from her mother's grasp and set her on the floor with some toys to play with. Then she enfolded her daughter in her arms and stroked her hair.

'I don't know, my love,' she said, 'but I know Someone who does. The Lord has us all in His hands…'

'But I sinned,' Joyce blurted out brokenly. 'I deliberately did what I did because I wanted to, and I knew it was wrong… And now I'm being punished…'

She pulled away from her mother and gazed into her eyes. 'I can't expect God to come to my rescue when I've ignored Him for so long and turned my back on Him. Just because I need help now, why should He help me? I don't deserve His help!'

Hannah Cormack smiled and took her daughter's hands in hers. 'That's exactly why you can expect God to help you,' she said. 'You know you've gone wrong, you've said so. You know you turned away from God, but you still know you need Him. This is you calling out to Him for forgiveness and help.'

Tears trickled through Joyce's tight-shut eyelids, but she nodded.

'God loves you,' Hannah said. 'He loves you regardless of what you've done, and He's glad that you still want to know Him. He loves to help His children. He just waits, impatiently, for them to realise that they need Him, need Him to come and rescue them, and then He's there – in action. Turning round horrible, hopeless situations. Bringing joy. Beauty from ashes.'

She paused. 'Maybe I never told you,' she murmured. 'Maybe I should have. But He certainly did that for me – and more than once.'

Joyce opened her eyes in surprise. 'Tell me.'

'Well, I've loved your father it seems since I was Georgie's age! But when your Aunt Belle couldn't get the man she wanted, she was determined to have your father – and keep him from me. She knew I loved him... When she was dying she said she'd make him vow never to remarry...'

'Oh that was cruel,' Joyce breathed.

'Yes,' her mother agreed calmly. 'It was. But God had other plans and Belle died before she could get the words out. Later, when it looked hopeless again, your brother Bobby stepped in – like an angel messenger. He brought us together, and your father and I were married.'

'Yes,' Joyce said. She knew that part of the story.

'But your father was still enslaved by Belle. I had his affection, respect... but not his love.'

'But Dad loves you!' Joyce protested.

'He does now,' Hannah agreed. 'But our marriage was a sham from the start, and close to disaster by 1914. Your father actually said to me that he should never have married me.'

Joyce gasped but Hannah continued. 'He went to the war to get away. And I think he hoped he might even be killed, ending our marriage in an honourable way.'

Tears glistened in her eyes.

'But it was not to be. God had other ideas.'

'What happened?' Joyce asked.

Hannah gazed back over the years and settled down to tell her daughter the story exactly as Rab had told her.

CHAPTER 48

Somewhere in France, 1915

Rab Cormack leaned against the wall of the trench, rifle in his hand, bayonet fixed at the ready, waiting for the order to go over the top.

As he waited, he pondered. So much of the time was spent waiting: waiting for orders, waiting to move, waiting for this, that and the other. And in all the time, very little seemed to be achieved – a few yards of muddy ground won, then the same few yards lost a couple of weeks later. Backwards and forwards they went, leaving behind their dead – men and horses – and the feet of those men that staggered past turned it into a more treacherous quagmire each time.

The worst of it was that the waiting provided plenty of time for thinking. And for those with loved ones at home, for writing letters. Rab was glad of the censorship and the form postcards handed out for them to use. Sending one of those at regular intervals was much easier than trying to write to Hannah.

In the months away from home, he had come face to face with himself in the raw here in France and he did not like what he saw. He had to admit that he had wronged Hannah – faithful Hannah who had never done anything in her life to hurt or harm him. As he waited in the grey clagging mud of the trench, he brought to mind Hannah's determinedly cheerful face. Yes, he knew: she had always loved him. And he had never loved her. She simply could not hold a candle to her sister. Belle. The beautiful one.

Rab sighed. Belle had captured his heart from the first time he saw her, and even in death, she held it still. He allowed his mind to run through his memories of Belle once again. It was a familiar, well-worn trail, each memory polished to a more glorious radiance from the reliving of it, over and over.

His lovely Belle. Why did she have to die and leave him? They could have been so happy! He would have done anything to make her happy! But it was not to be. A cruel fate had taken her away. And the ever-present Hannah had stepped matter-of-factly into the breach, seeing to the child whose birth had killed Belle, and to his needs.

All his needs. There was a baby son back at home to prove that. But there was no love in him for Hannah.

Rab shifted uncomfortably. These past years, as Hannah had loved him and served him and made him comfortable, he had been living a lie and as the years went by he saw the glow – the hope – maybe even the love – vanish from Hannah's face. Slowly, the light dimmed and she went from being a radiantly happy bride to a determined, loyal, hard-working… unloved wife.

It had been past time to get out. Rab squinted over the top of the trench. This war had come at just the right moment for him. It had given him an honourable way to get himself out of her life and their uncomfortable marriage. Not that she ever said anything. But he could see her sadness. Her disappointment.

That last conversation when he had put it into words: 'I should never have married you.' That had been the final nail in the coffin of their marriage – their marriage that had never had a chance from the start.

A shout alerted him. It was time to get himself up and out of the trench, across No-Man's Land, and confront the enemy.

Around him, the bullets started flying. Rab did not care. Somewhere there was a bullet with his name on it and he would welcome its coming. Hannah, if she had any honesty – and he was sure she did – would also welcome it.

And the telegram that said he had died honourably in battle – that would set her free from a very bad bargain.

CHAPTER 49

Eyes focused on the enemy lines up ahead, Rab forced his way forward, diving for cover as a fusillade of enemy fire came too close, then pulling himself back to his feet and joining the onward push again.

Screaming. Shouting. The roar of heavy guns. The slithering struggle of booted feet through the ankle-deep mud.

Suddenly, the ground went from under him and Rab found himself at the bottom of a deep shell hole, lying spread-eagled on his back, gazing up at the sky. Above him, his comrades fought their way forward, none sparing even a glance down the shell hole.

Rab stared at the wall in front of him. It was high and smooth with nothing to provide a hand-hold. He would have to dig his heels and his bayonet in to prise himself out. Cautiously he got himself to his knees. Quickly checking, he appeared to have taken no damage. But a sudden groan alerted him to the fact that he was not alone.

He took a firm grip on his rifle – for protection, he told himself. If his companion was a German, he did not want to kill him, but then again, he was not keen on being a sitting duck himself! Rab looked around him. There huddled in the corner of the pit, the muddied khaki of his uniform blending with the wall behind him, was a British soldier – from the flash on his sleeve, an officer.

'Sir?' Rab said tentatively.

The groan was repeated.

Rab shuffled on his knees across to the man.

'Sir?' he asked again.

The officer opened pain-clouded eyes. He seemed to take a moment to steady himself.

'Do I know you?' he asked in an Edinburgh accent.

'No, sir,' Rab said. 'Do you need help?'

'Help?' the officer echoed, appearing to drift off for a moment. Then his eyes refocused. 'I rather think I'm beyond help.' He gestured to his leg and Rab saw a filthy makeshift bandage soaked in blood. 'I was shot, fell in here, and with this… Well, you can see for yourself I can't get out.' He raised his head, listening. Rab listened too. Above them the battle raged.

'You might as well make yourself comfortable,' the officer said with a wry smile. 'I think we're here for a while. Go on. At ease. There's just the two of us.'

Rab grinned and hunkered down beside the officer. 'Is there anything I can do?'

The man gestured at his bandage. 'You could have a go at doing something better with that. You'd have thought I'd be better with my hands!' He laughed. 'In civvie street, I worked with my hands and I was good at my job, but I haven't made much of a fist of this!'

Rab knelt beside him and began to untie the makeshift bandage carefully. The wound was deep and had shattered the bone. The man must be in dreadful pain. The flash of a hip flask put swiftly to the man's lips told Rab how he was dealing with it.

'D'you want a drink?' the office asked. 'I don't have much left.'

'Thank you kindly, sir,' Rab answered. 'But I rather think you're in more need of it than me, and anyway I'm not much of a drinker.'

'Where are you from?' the officer asked. 'You accent sounds a wee bit familiar...'

'I'm a Wicker,' Rab said, his head bent to the task of rebinding the bandage round the man's ruined leg.

'Is that so?' A smile ghosted the officer's lips. 'I once knew someone from Wick. A young lady – well, she wasn't a lady, if you take my meaning?' He glanced with amusement at Rab. 'It was before I was married.'

Rab nodded. Bandage firmly tied, it would do till he could get the officer out of there and off to the field hospital. The noise above them told him it would be a while yet before he could try to get them out. It would be best to keep the officer's mind occupied. *Keep him talking*, Rab thought.

'Oh aye,' Rab said. 'That would have been in Edinburgh?'

'Yes, indeed. You heard that in my accent, did you?' the officer asked, darting a quick glance Rab's way. 'Smart man. Ah well, they're smart folk in Wick. Well, at least she thought she was.' Again the reminiscent smile. 'But in the end I was too smart for her.'

He cocked his head to listen to the battle above him. 'We're probably just as well out of it,' he said, then picking up the conversation added, 'Yes, I'm from Edinburgh. I'm Adam Finlayson. And you are?'

'Rab Cormack,' Rab answered immediately, though Adam's name had tugged his memory. He had heard the name before, a long time ago, but where?

CHAPTER 50

'You've heard my name?' The officer puffed out his chest. 'Ah well, that's not surprising. I took over my father's business and built it into the biggest in the city.' He waved at his ruined leg. 'If we can get out of here alive, with luck this will get me sent back home where I belong.'

His eyes glazed as he drifted in pain and memory. With an effort he reached into his tunic pocket and pulled out a battered photograph. He held it out to Rab.

'The wife and bairns,' he said proudly. He pointed at the picture. 'That's my son, Will. And the wee girl, Meggie, is as pretty as her mother.' He sighed. 'I did well when I married her... She's a fine woman and has been a great help in my career.' He squinted up at Rab. 'But it put paid to any fun and games,' he added, ruefully shaking his head. 'I've walked the straight and narrow since we married. I hardly recognise myself!'

Rab joined dutifully in his laughter. There had not been much 'fun and games', as Adam Finlayson put it, in his life – though he remembered fleetingly the wonder of Belle's generous, surprising welcome that last time he had arrived in Edinburgh to visit her.

'Belle...'

But it was not her name on *his* lips but on Adam's. Rab's head jerked upright and he stared at the man.

'Ah yes, my last little fling before I married! Pretty Belle from Wick. You'd probably know her, a girl like that?' Adam asked with cheerful assurance.

Rab's throat constricted. It couldn't be *his* Belle the man was talking about... But now the vague familiarity of Adam Finlayson's name grew stronger. Was that not the name of the man who had taken advantage of Belle and broken her heart, sending her headlong into his grateful arms? Fierce anger began to surge in him.

But Adam was still speaking. 'Ah, she was a lot of fun, was Belle, and no coy tricks about her. That was the best thing. She knew what she wanted and she went after it straight like an arrow from a bow.' He shook his head in amusement. 'But the silly girl thought she could have me! She thought once I'd tasted her wares, I'd want to keep her. Well, I might have, as my mistress, but a man in my position doesn't marry a girl like that.'

The words pounded on Rab's ears. 'Mistress'. 'No coy tricks'. 'Tasted her wares'. 'A girl like that'. Each word, each phrase battered at his picture of his Belle. Surely this could not be his lovely Belle? There must be some mistake.

His Belle had gone to Edinburgh to keep her widowed aunt company. While she was there, she had worked in a high-class tailoring company until the owner's son had tried to take advantage of her and broken her heart. It had been an amazing providence, Rab remembered, that had led him across her path that very day. He recalled how Belle had sobbed into his shoulder and allowed him to comfort her... Sheepishly, he remembered the hasty proposal of marriage and their return home to Wick, newly engaged.

'In the end she overplayed her hand,' Adam Finlayson was saying. 'She thought she had me where she wanted me – and what she wanted was marriage and to rule the roost at the business.' He paused and explained, 'I run a tailoring business – the best in Edinburgh.'

Rab stared at him. Tailoring business? Was it possible that this man was the one who had so cruelly deceived Belle? But the story Adam was telling was very different from the one that Belle had told him.

Rab shook his head, trying to clear the confusion that threatened to overpower him. Of all the men in the world he had to fall into a shell hole beside, this was the man from the tailoring establishment in Edinburgh where Belle had worked. But whose story was the truth: Belle's or Adam's? Rab listened in rising horror.

'I thought I handled the end of it rather well,' Adam said smugly. 'She thought she was pregnant – I know that. But I wasn't going to get caught in that trap. I offered her money, pretending I was paying her off. I knew she wouldn't tolerate that insult. She thought she was better than the trollops on the street! So off she went in high dudgeon. I was able to marry my Margaret. I heard later Belle managed to snaffle some poor gullible soul who probably thought the baby was his, if I know my Belle! She'd have got him into bed with her so fast he wouldn't be thinking straight enough to count on his fingers!'

Adam Finlayson lay back against the muddy pit wall and laughed. And his words and his laughter were like buckets of ice water. Each damning word struck Rab with searing clarity. His Belle had tried to entrap Adam Finlayson and then when he turned her off, she had opened her arms to him when he had arrived unexpectedly in Edinburgh. Unexpectedly but oh, so conveniently for her. Rab remembered how, in a whirlwind haze of what he had thought was love, he had been securely netted.

They had come straight back to Wick and announced their engagement. The wedding had followed soon after. Belle had lost the baby, Rab remembered. Bobby, though, was definitely his. Rab knew that for sure. He could count on his fingers, no matter how big a fool he had been. And now with anguish, he realised he had indeed been a fool, blinded by his love for Belle. Or had it been love?

A sudden picture came to him of Hannah, standing apron-clad in his kitchen in the days after Belle's death. Hannah quietly coming and providing food, cleaning up the place, seeing to his laundry. Looking after the baby. All those thankless years.

Now that was love. Hannah's steadfast, loyal love that asked for nothing for herself. Not the star-struck dazzlement he had felt for Belle. That was infatuation. Lust.

He looked at Adam Finlayson, lying cheerfully in the mud, his story told. With death close at his door, he had no need to tell lies.

'*And ye shall know the truth, and the truth shall make you free.*'²˙

The text came suddenly into Rab's mind and he knew he had been given his freedom. Out here in a muddy shell hole in No-Man's Land. God had opened his eyes and set him free.

And instead of his first rage and the ugly need to silence the man as Adam told what was only the unvarnished truth about the woman who had tried to manipulate the pair of them, Rab suddenly felt a strange urge to embrace the man and thank him.

---

2   ˙ John 8:32

CHAPTER 51

Rab found himself smiling ruefully. It was not Adam Finlayson he needed to embrace but Hannah. Hannah who had loved him all these years. And as he thought of Hannah, he recognised a deep warm glow of gratitude for her, and a longing to see her again, to try to put things right, to love her as she had loved him. If only it was not too late...

He realised that around them there was silence. The exchanges of gunfire and shelling had stopped. The battlefield was quiet.

Maybe they could get out of here. Maybe he could survive this terrible war and get home to Hannah and start again.

'Shall we take our chances?' he asked Adam Finlayson.

'If you'll help me,' Adam said. 'I'm willing to give it a go.'

Rab gave him a hand to get him up on his one good leg. Then clawing in the mud, hauling and pushing Adam, slowly Rab managed to get the pair of them out of the shell hole.

They lay side by side on the edge, surrounded by the eerie silence of No-Man's Land, panting for breath.

'You knew her.' Adam made it a simple statement.

'Aye, I knew her,' Rab said, his eyes searching for the best route back to Allied lines.

He turned to see Adam's eyes questioning.

'I was the poor fool she trapped after you,' Rab said shortly. 'I'd always thought I loved her – and that she loved me. That you'd seduced her, led her astray...'

Adam's laughter blew away the last faint wisps of lingering illusion.

'So why didn't you kill me, down in the pit?' Adam asked. 'No one would have known. Or you could simply have left me there.'

'No, sir,' Rab said. '*I* would have known and *God* would have known. In any case, you've done me a mighty service today. You've opened my eyes and set me free.'

'She died in childbirth. No, not *your* child,' he answered Adam's startled question. 'She miscarried that one early on. No, this is my son, Bobby. He's a fine lad. But she died and I have mourned her and carried her memory heavy on my heart ever since. What you've told me today has taken that load from me and set me free. And now it's my turn to repay you.'

He checked around them.

'Let's be going.'

And he seized Adam in a firm grip and started out for the front line.

'You'd do better without me,' Adam panted, half an hour later. German snipers had spotted them making their painful way across the barren wastes and they were once more face-down in the mud, trying to make as small a target of themselves as possible.

'I am not leaving you,' Rab told him forcefully. 'Right,' he said rising to a crouch. 'Get your arm across my shoulder and we'll hunker down and do it like a couple of crabs scuttling for the shore!'

Adam laughed weakly, though the blood was soaking through his trouser leg again and his strength was all but gone.

'One more try,' Rab said and began the last stage of their journey. 'Nearly there!'

'Well done,' Adam murmured, then slumped into unconsciousness, a deadweight on Rab's shoulder. Another bullet whistled close by. Rab crouched, waiting, then in a final desperate surge of strength, he pulled Adam across his shoulders, rose up and ran across the final furlongs to the Allied lines.

A watcher called, 'Over here!' and Rab, blinded by sweat and exhaustion, staggered the final yards to the edge of the trench.

Hands appeared from below to take Adam from him, and Rab rose to slide him off his shoulder. As he slumped, the deadweight gone, he felt the sudden terrible impact of a bullet and blacked out.

His last thought was of Hannah. Despairingly, he cried out to her. Would he never get home to tell her he loved her?

CHAPTER 52

'Rab took a bullet on his way back to the British lines,' Hannah continued the story. 'His time in the field hospital gave him time to think, and by the time he came home, he was a different man.'

She thought back to the hesitant, war-weary, wounded man who had turned up unexpectedly that summer afternoon.

The telegram announcing that Rab was missing in action, presumed dead, had cut her to the quick, but she had determined to trust her Lord and wait in quiet dependence on Him. Then at last the news had come that Rab was alive but wounded.

She had waited then. She remembered Bobby playing with young Danny in the garden. Dear Bobby, at eighteen so grown-up and proud of his job with a local car-hire firm, yet willing to play with his much younger half-brother.

Their shouts of delight were music to her ears and she had opened her book to read contentedly on that lovely afternoon. But suddenly she realised she could no longer see or hear the boys in the garden. She rose and went determinedly to the door to see what those rascals were up to now.

But before she reached it, a man stood there, filling the frame with his tall, beloved presence. He looked tired, and his eyes searched hers as if unsure of his welcome.

'Rab!' Hannah cried and his arms opened to engulf her in a rib-cracking embrace.

'Hannah!' he murmured. 'Oh Hannah, I have wasted so much time...'

The clamour of the boys drove them apart. 'Dad's home!'

It was only when, at last, they were alone together, that Rab was able to tell all and hesitantly to ask Hannah if she would give him another chance... a chance at a marriage rooted this time in love.

Tears came to her eyes now as she remembered. She brushed them away as she gazed at her daughter, her Joyce, the expression of their loving reunion and the joy they had found in one another.

'Oh my dear,' Hannah said. 'No marriage is easy, but I fear you, like your father, may have been deceived.'

Joyce stared at her mother.

'Your father was duped – deliberately – by Belle. Lured into marriage.' Her mother's grey eyes fixed on hers. 'Like you, I think.'

Joyce shook her head. Surely she had not been duped? Her pregnancy had been an accident, hadn't it? A mistake. She tried to think back, but her mind was fuzzy with confusion.

Hannah looked steadily into Joyce's eyes.

'I think it's time we take your situation to the Lord. And if you need to come home, my dear, there will be no questions asked. We'll gladly take you and the little one in. You'll be safe with us. I promise you.'

CHAPTER 53

George tossed back the last of his whisky. He dragged himself to his feet and threw his raincoat on over his dark blue chauffeur's suit. The conversation around him quietened. He liked that. Respect. Maybe this was only a small town on the edge of nowhere, but he was still a man to be reckoned with. He gave a mirthless grin and looked round the room with satisfaction.

It was he who provided the illicit whisky that stood on each of the tables. This shebeen and the several others like it might only be run-down cottages on quiet side streets of the town, but the owners were beholden to George and he was beginning to make a satisfactory return on his investments.

But it was becoming more difficult to balance the demands of his illicit activities with continuing to play the hard-working son-in-law. Worse, the lucrative Cormack business seemed just as far as ever out of his reach, and his patience was fast wearing thin.

Why couldn't Joyce have given birth to a boy? George's fingers clenched in anger. That would have solved everything. A son and heir for Rab Cormack to pass the business down to. But now, though the Cormacks were pleased enough with Georgie (though not,

George recalled with a spiteful smile, with her middle name, Belle!), her arrival had not brought him any closer to control of the business – and the money it brought in. Money he wanted to get his hands on sooner rather than later.

And if he was not mistaken, the façade of his marriage was beginning to show its cracks. To forestall any awkward questions about her bruises, he had told Joyce she must stay at home and look after the child and there was to be no gadding about. He had put about tales of the child's ill health as cover. He had no wish for Joyce to spill any unwelcome beans.

But there had been something different in her demeanour these last few days, something he could not quite put his finger on. Yes, she was still pleasingly afraid of him and jumped at his every word. But… there was just something in the way she was. A little of that stillness her mother had. It was unsettling.

He would have to deal with it. There was no room for anyone or anything rocking the boat.

Mr Cormack seemed to be watching him ever more closely these days too. Slipping away to check on his customers in the shebeens was becoming more difficult. Maybe he was imagining it, George told himself crossly. He had been careful, and everyone involved in the sale and purchase of illegal drink knew to keep quiet. And George was very careful to maintain – in public – a safe distance from Ruby. He made sure he went about his work at the garage with his usual apparent diligence.

But something just did not feel right. So what could the problem be? The only weakness he could see in the whole situation was Joyce. If she had said anything…

With sudden decision, he put on his hat, turned up the collar of his coat and stalked out of the shebeen, heading for home. He was supposed to be out on a hire. She would not be expecting him. All the better…

~

George let himself into the house quietly and stood in the hallway listening. There was only silence. Surely Joyce had not gone out – without his permission? He waited. Then very faintly he detected movement upstairs, in the bedroom.

At this time of day? What would she be doing up there at this time? He knew what he would be doing if it were him! But surely Joyce had not taken a lover? The idea was laughable! Poor downtrodden, pale-faced Joyce, a shadow of the insipidly pretty girl she had once been – no man would look twice at her!

He heard her voice, cooing… to the child! Ah yes, that was probably it. She would be changing the baby. But wait, the child was surely past nappies and all that. He had not taken much notice of these things. They were her job. But yes, surely, at age three, Georgie was out of nappies and had no need of changing?

So what was going on? Perhaps the child had had an accident, spilt something and needed a change of clothing… George brushed it away. It was of no interest.

Then he realised Joyce was singing. It was a long time since he had heard her singing. She sounded happy, her voice young and clear. Fury boiled up in him. What had she to be happy about? *Had* she taken a lover? How dare she!

Swiftly and silently he took the stairs to the landing, then stopped stock still. Their bedroom door was open and Joyce was standing by the bed singing as she packed clothes into an open suitcase. Drawers stood open. And she was singing. Happy and singing.

'What are you doing?' George ground out.

Joyce jumped, sudden terror in her face. The singing stopped abruptly.

'George!' she stammered. 'What are you doing here?'

He strode across the hallway into the bedroom and grabbed her by the shoulders, glaring into her face at close quarters.

'It's my home, isn't it?' he said. 'Why shouldn't I be here?'

'But... But... you were on a hire, to...'

'Oh yes,' he said. 'You thought I was out of the way.'

Guilt flooded Joyce's face.

George shook her roughly. 'So what are you doing? Answer me!'

In a sudden unexpected movement, Joyce pulled away from his grasp. She moved to the other side of the bed, with the suitcase between them.

'I'm leaving you,' she said, with trembling bravery. 'I'm packing, and I'm going. Home to my mother. Today. Me and Georgie.'

George's eyes narrowed. If Joyce left, all his efforts to get his hands on the Cormack business – and the Cormack money – would come to nothing. He would be thrown out as soon as she poured out her story to her parents. If she had not done so already.

He would have to start over again. The pictures flickered through his mind – Buenos Aires, Chicago, the penitentiary, Glasgow, and now this little grey town, Ruby and the shebeen, and the Cormack business he had so nearly got his hands on...

'And you can't stop me!' the girl said with new defiance.

Her words hit him hard. Rage poured red and hot through his mind. Where was the respect he deserved? He would show her!

In an instant he was round the bed, his open hand slamming against her face.

Joyce gasped but did not back away.

Infuriated, George seized her by her hair and dragged her to her knees. He stood over her.

'I can't stop you?' he demanded.

But Joyce was not cowed. Tears of pain were in her eyes and fear in her face, but still she managed to shake her head.

'No,' she said. 'No! I've made up my mind. You can't make me change my mind. You can hurt me as much as you like but...'

Her words were the final straw.

'I'll hurt you,' George swore at her as he dragged her from the floor onto the bed, pushing her down over the open suitcase and ignoring her protests as he pushed her clothes aside, tearing and clawing in his mindless fury to overpower her, intent on punishing her, vanquishing her.

As Joyce realised what George intended, she tried to protest, to plead, to fight, but his strength was too great, his anger too overpowering. And when he was finished and threw her from him, she lay beaten, sobbing amidst the ruins of her clothes.

'Daddy?' a voice from the doorway interrupted them.

Joyce looked aghast at George. How much had the child witnessed?

George turned away to rearrange his clothing, then he turned back and spoke to his daughter.

'Bad girls have to be punished. Your mummy has been bad... But she'll be good now.'

He turned back to Joyce.

'Won't you?'

CHAPTER 54

'Pregnant? What do you mean she's pregnant again?' Ruby screeched. 'You told me you never touched her any more!'

'It was a one-off,' George said. Then with his temper rising, he added 'And in any case, it's got nothing to do with you.' What was he doing: explaining himself to a woman?

Ruby planted herself in front of him, arms akimbo.

'Well, I think it's got a lot to do with me. I'm your partner and you need to keep on the right side of me. You know if I blow the whistle, that will be the end of all your money-making schemes. And Mr respectable Cormack will throw you out, new baby or no new baby!'

George drew in a sharp angry breath. Yes, Ruby knew too much. He could not afford to alienate her.

His eyes narrowed. Perhaps she knew too much for her own good? If she had become a liability, or was determined to be a threat…

'Don't even think about it,' Ruby said shrewdly, and laughed. 'Oh, come on, Georgie-Porgie! We're two of a kind, and we're better off together than apart.'

Bitterly, he had to admit she was right. She was the only woman who ever stood up to him, laughed at him, entertained him and never bored him. She could give as good as she got. But for the time being he would have to keep his nose clean – and make sure she caused no problems for him.

If only Joyce would produce a boy child this time! He was sure that was the key to the Cormack business – and the Cormack coffers. And the sooner he had that securely in his hands, the better. There were too many rumblings in Wick about rescinding the decision for the town to be dry. If that happened, his main source of income would vanish overnight.

He could not afford for Ruby to threaten his security. She was becoming increasingly demanding. And bored. Could he keep her sweet for the next six months?

'You're right,' he told her, with what he hoped was a charming grin. Her response told him she knew him too well and could see through it. He threw up his hands in surrender. 'All right, I tell you what. You just stay home here with your mother in Lybster for a little while longer, being a good little girl. No more trips to Wick. And I don't want to see you at your uncle's shebeen.'

She glared at him.

'I need to play my part for a while yet… till this child is born. If it's a boy, I need the will changed so the garage business goes to the child. Then I can deal with the Cormacks. Mr Cormack isn't getting any younger and his health is not good. With him out of the way…'

Ruby's eyes widened. 'You would do that?'

George shrugged. 'He may need a little help. It's not a problem.' He thought of the men he had helped on their way in Chicago and Glasgow. What was one more? Except, of course, that it would need to be done more discreetly.

Perhaps a motor accident? George pondered. He had spent quite a bit of his time in the garage workshop in his early days and was a competent mechanic. It would not take much to engineer a small, fatal accident.

'So you be a good girl,' he told Ruby, 'for a little while yet.'

Her eyes told him she was not appeased.

'Our time will come,' George said. 'Believe me.'

CHAPTER 55

Langwell, Caithness, 1943

The men swarmed down off the lorries and gazed around at the place that would be their home for the foreseeable future. After the past two years at the camp at Lamington Park, this place was more rugged and much more beautiful – if you had an eye for such things.

The Québécois lads were chattering away in French as they unloaded their kit bags. Even this high up in the Highlands, the July sun was hot as they got themselves sorted out.

It was as well that he was used to quiet places, Hugh thought. Some of the other lads craved the bright lights and night life of cities. Here, they were miles from the nearest town – and a small one at that.

Was it coincidence that of all the places in Scotland the Corps had been deployed, his unit should have been sent to Caithness, the very county his father came from, he wondered. Or was it at last a blessing from the God his beloved mother believed so firmly in?

'He will look after you,' had been her parting words to him. 'If you'll let Him!'

She knew him so well, knew he had given up on God when Katie died. Hugh shrugged. It did not matter. God or no God, he had wanted a change of scene and he had got it.

Enlisting in the Canadian Forestry Corps had been easy. There had been mobilisation centres in every province as the Government sought to put together around twenty companies of foresters and related trades to help the war effort in Britain. Hugh had discovered that Papa Bill's insistence that he work with the men clearing virgin land of trees, and then processing them at the old sawmill on the ranch, had once again come in handy and he found himself almost instantly promoted to Sergeant. Other men in his group had been loggers, blacksmiths, mechanics and cooks in civilian life and they too were welcomed into the ranks.

The Corps were to fight in the war in mainland Europe if necessary, so Hugh was sent with his fellows to Quebec for military training, and then with the rest of No. 9 Company, he had embarked at Halifax for the Atlantic crossing in convoy.

They had disembarked on the Clyde in the spring of 1941. The heavy industrial landscape blasted by heavy German bombing had come as a shock to Hugh who had expected Scotland to be wild and beautiful and blooming with spring flowers. But once they were loaded onto trains for their journey north, the countryside soon became more like the Scotland of his imagination.

'Dear Hugo,' he had written to his son. 'Well, I'm here. Because of war rules, I'm not allowed to tell you exactly where I am but there are lots of trees and hills.'

He tried to write to Hugo every week, sending him humorous stories of his work in the Scottish forests. The Québécois were a great crowd, hard-working and generous with their friendship. Hugh was glad that Mama Marie had insisted he learn French from her. Half

French, half native Canadian, she had been proud of her heritage – and Hugh was grateful now for the language lessons which enabled him to chat comfortably with his comrades in arms.

'*Hope you're enjoying school and making the most of it,*' Hugh always ended his letters.

Hugo had managed to get into the school of his choice where he could sit the exams he needed. Holiday times he returned to stay with his grandmother Nancy in her little house in town.

'Eh, you not hungry?'

It was Benoit, one of his friends in the Corps. 'Time to eat, yeah?'

Hugh hurriedly folded the letter and tucked it into his battledress pocket. He would finish it later.

He rose and joined Benoit at the cookhouse.

CHAPTER 56

Lybster

'He never?' Ruby exclaimed.

'He did,' Ruby's cousin May insisted. 'It went something like this.' She took a breath and put on a plummy pretend-posh English accent: *'The Canadians arriving in your midst will not be of much help in your war effort. Lock up your daughters and stay off the roads. Give these men a motorcycle and a bottle of whisky and they will kill themselves.'*

'That Lord Haw-Haw!' Ruby said dismissively. 'What does he know?'

'Well, he knew about the Canadians coming to Blair Atholl,' May said. She had been posted there as a Land Girl for the past year. Then she added with a sly grin, 'And *you'll* find out soon enough if what he says about them is true!'

'Why? What's happening?' Ruby asked, eyes bright with curiosity.

'There are Canadians down at Berriedale, even as we speak. I expect they've come to cut down the trees at Langwell.'

'There never are!' Ruby grinned, catching her cousin's teasing mood.

'I saw a timber lorry with some Canadians in it from the bus as we went round that corner just at the bottom of the hill into Berriedale,' May said with delight.

'How do you know they're Canadians?' Ruby demanded. 'They could have been anybody!'

'They were in uniform, silly,' her cousin told her. 'And they've got green cap badges with a tree and Canadian Forestry Corps in big capital letters on it! Once you've seen it, you won't mistake it.'

The girls drank their tea in silence while Ruby digested her cousin's news.

'So how long is your leave?' she asked May.

'I've got another two days, then I've got to get back,' May grinned at her cousin. 'It's hard work but good fun!'

'I wish I could do something,' Ruby mused. 'I am so bored here but they won't take women with children. And the in-laws won't hear of me going back to work... "not while the child is so young..." She repeated what Mrs Cormack had said just the other day when she had raised the question once again. 'Makes me feel trapped. "A child needs her mother..." as if I didn't know!'

'How old is Amanda now?' May enquired.

'She's three.'

'She's a good little thing.'

'Yes,' Ruby agreed. 'She's no trouble at all.'

'Couldn't you leave her with your mum and volunteer for something?'

Ruby sighed. 'What sort of thing?'

'Well, after the Bignold Hospital at Wick was bombed, they moved everything here to Lybster, didn't they? That's where all the patients are now.'

Ruby nodded.

'Well, you could help there – visit the patients, take tea round, roll bandages...'

'What, me?' Ruby asked in disbelief. 'Do the gracious lady of mercy bit? Are you joking?'

Her cousin shrugged. 'Suit yourself. But just think... All those handsome officers, helpless in bed, and you come along, all kind and appealing...' May laughed as Ruby considered the picture she had painted. 'Go on. It might be fun! And hospitals are always desperate for help.'

'Yes, but... *me*?' Ruby said.

'What they don't know won't hurt them,' her cousin said robustly. 'And they're in no position to quibble. If you volunteer, they've pretty well got to take you. Dress up all demure – do the tragic young widow in your blacks. Try and look as respectable as you can...'

She laughed at the horror in Ruby's face.

'Well, the first time anyway!' May encouraged. 'All you need to do is leave off the lipstick and find a hat you can stuff your hair into so you look prim and proper. Then you can ease up and be yourself once you've got yourself in there.'

'Mmm,' Ruby pondered. 'It's a thought. Maybe I will give it a try. A couple of mornings a week – that would do nicely. Mum wouldn't mind looking after Amanda. It would get me out of the house. And it would look good for my boring in-laws.'

'You still need to keep in with them?' May queried curiously.

'Yes,' Ruby said shortly. 'They pay the bills.'

Admittedly George paid for the little extras that made life pleasant, but there was no need to tell her cousin that. She did not want her getting ideas – or meeting George! Maybe the sooner May was back down the road to her posting in Blair Atholl, the better.

But on Monday, *she* would be presenting herself for volunteer duties at the hospital.

CHAPTER 57

George laughed when he heard.

'You'll never stick it!' he said as Ruby told him about her new duties at the hospital. 'Rolling bandages? Handing out cups of tea? You'll have had enough of that in no time.'

Ruby hid a smile. Little did he know what fun she was already having at the hospital. The injured men on the wards appreciated her cheerful presence. She brightened up their lives. And they brightened up hers.

He kissed her perfunctorily on the cheek and headed back to the car tucked safely round the corner. It was still a bone of contention between them but George was adamant. His visits to Ruby had to be curtailed for the time being in the light of the Cormacks' less-than-approving vigilance.

Once the new baby was born – once he had provided a son and heir for the Cormack business – all would be well. But first he had to continue playing the role of the loving husband and dutiful son-in-law.

Joyce, fortunately, had been easy to deal with.

'I don't know what came over me!' George had cried and flung himself at her feet. 'Will you ever forgive me? This child – our child – should be a child of love like...'

For a moment he faltered as 'Amanda' – the wrong name – hovered on his lips. He caught it in time and managed to remember 'Georgina'. After all, the child was named after him!

'Oh *mi cariño*, how can I ever make it up to you?'

He had buried his head in her lap and waited. Joyce had sat stiffly, but as his words poured out, he could feel her unbend and at last her hand came down on his shoulder, a gentle touch at first, hesitant, then firmer. He had dared to look up at her then, keeping his face tortured with remorse.

'Oh my darling,' Joyce had said. 'Of course I forgive you.'

He had shaken his head. 'No! No! How can you? What I did... It was unforgivable! I am so sorry...' He had lapsed into Spanish then, knowing that she would not understand a word.

Her hand had gripped his shoulder.

'No, my love, you must not torture yourself so. It is past. We will put it behind us. We love one another...' She had looked to him for confirmation and he had readily given her the assurance she sought.

'You alone,' he pledged. 'You are my only love!'

She had bent her head and kissed him gently, first on his forehead, then softly, daringly, on his lips.

He had answered with a passion that delighted her. George, observing the role he was playing, was satisfied. He had got away with it. But from now on he would have to play happy families.

But not for ever. No. Not for ever.

CHAPTER 58

'*Dear Hugo,*

We have moved. From one Scottish forest to another. This one has the best larch any of us have seen and we have plenty of work cutting down the trees and processing them in the sawmills. We've got all our kit here now – tractors, sulkies, winches, the mobile mills – but we also use the Scotch mill or bench down by the river. It's a hazardous thing because you have to push the log by hand towards the saw. We haven't got the generator fixed up at the camp yet but we're managing fine.

It's a very beautiful place, more rugged than the last. There are two good salmon rivers and the lads have enjoyed a spot of fishing. There's black game up at one of the other sites and they're good eating. I saw a golden eagle the other day.'

What else to tell him? Hugh tried to imagine Hugo reading the letter, sharing it with friends at his school. He felt a pang of homesickness for Hugo and Canada, and quickly suppressed it. He had chosen to come here. He had wanted to get away.

He continued writing.

'*The locals are very welcoming and we've been invited to dances and parties at the local hall. We've even been included in a celebration*

206

for the local doctor who has served the area for 44 years! That was at Dunbeath, where he is based.'

The censor would probably strike that name out, but if it got through, it would have Hugo poring over an atlas to find out where exactly his father had been posted.

'It's not far away and he comes over to see us two or three times a week. There is always the odd injury needing attention.

As at the last place, we're divided into two sections, one cutting in the bush and bringing out the timber on the sulkies, the other sawing it into useable lumber ready for transportation. Those Scotch mills are not as good as ours, but without the generator in place we have no choice but to use it.

The locals are interested in our equipment. It's more modern than anything they've got and the caterpillar tractors have come in handy a couple of times to help out locals bogged down in the snow and ice on the steep hills.

Apart from the work, the social events, and a little poaching, life goes on here very quietly. We hike in the hills. Some men cycle to Wick or Helmsdale – the two nearest towns. I haven't bothered yet, but I may try to go in the next week when I have a few days' leave.'

Though what he would do when he had the free time, he did not know. Let his hair down a little, maybe? Compared to some of the men in No. 9 Company he was still comparatively young. And who knew when they would be sent to France to fight?

Life was short. You had to make the most of it.

CHAPTER 59

'It was all a mistake!' Joyce protested.

Her mother fixed her eyes on her, those steady grey eyes under whose gaze Joyce faltered.

'Are you sure, my dear?' Hannah Cormack asked gently.

Joyce's bent head, the dark hair hiding her face, nodded vehemently.

'I'm sure, Mum.'

She looked up and there were tears shining in her eyes.

'I love him! I really do!' She caught her mother's look then and added, 'Yes, I know. We went through a rough patch. But that's not unusual, is it? You said you and Dad had a rough patch.'

Hannah nodded thoughtfully.

Joyce rushed on. 'Men often… get their noses put out-of-joint when there's a new baby. That's all it was. And I'm not perfect!' She tried for a laugh. 'You know that!'

Her mother smiled but the smile did not reach her eyes.

'You know, if things were ever to get bad again…' she began.

'They won't, Mum,' Joyce assured her. 'George is a changed man. He's being wonderful. He helps with Georgie. She adores him!' She bit her lip. 'And so do I,' she added.

Her mother nodded thoughtfully. 'I'm glad to hear it, but just in case… If ever you feel you need to, you know you can always come home. You don't have to say anything. Just come.'

Joyce tried to stifle the horror her mother's words evoked in her. The memory of George's brutal rape had scarred her deeply. But then she remembered his contrite tears. No man – least of all a proud man like George – could fake such remorse!

And in the wake of that terrible incident, he had become the loving husband she had hoped for. He was attentive, looking after her and little Georgie so protectively, so lovingly. And he was so concerned for her and her pregnancy. Nothing was too much trouble! No matter what silly cravings she had, it seemed he would move heaven and earth to procure whatever she wanted.

She smiled at her mother more confidently.

'No truly, Mum,' she said. 'Everything's all right.'

The only slight cloud on her horizon was Ruby. She had always wondered whether there had ever been anything between George and Ruby. When Ruby had gone to live with her mother in Lybster after Bobby was killed in France, Joyce had wondered whether George was too keen to take on the ambulance trips out there after the Bignold Hospital moved to the Lybster school premises.

She shook her head. She would not think about such a thing. George was the perfect loving husband. How could she ever doubt him?

CHAPTER 60

'*I have exciting news!*' Hugh wrote with a grin. He imagined Hugo sitting up and taking notice. What had his intrepid father been up to now?

'*I won a prize at the monthly whist drive held at the Portland Hall by the Women's Rural Institute.*'

Hugh laughed out loud as he imagined the faces of Hugo and his friends at this news. He leaned back against the heathery bank and breathed in the soft Highland air. The headland where he sat fell steeply down to a sparkling blue sea. The ruins of Berriedale Castle crowned great craggy lumps of rock sticking out into the bay. In front of that natural barrier, the peaty brown water of one of the finest salmon rivers he had ever encountered pooled quietly beside a shingle beach. White-painted cottages stood on either side, with only a precarious swing bridge to join them.

It was a lovely place and Hugh was enjoying his 48-hour furlough. He had thought to get the bus into one of the towns to explore, but in the end, like most of the Company, he had chosen to stay close to camp. He enjoyed the wild scenery and it was a pleasure to hike and wander at will. Yesterday he had taken himself off to visit some of the local villages – Latheron, Latheronwheel, Dunbeath – far enough on a bicycle for a man of his age! And he made sure he returned in time for the big event.

The hospitality – and the baking! – of the Women's Rural Institute was legendary and every month a whist drive was held which included an excellent tea. It was a bright point in everyone's calendar. There was always a dance afterwards and the Forestry Corps provided the music – and welcome male partners – and everybody had a good time.

But this was the first time Hugh had won anything at the whist drive. He smiled with contentment. Maybe his luck was turning!

He puffed quietly on a cigarette. It would soon be time to go back to camp, but the peaceful sunlit bay made him want to stay. He could understand men who deserted – and the lads who married local girls and planned to return to settle here when the war was over.

When he was a child, being educated at home at the ranch, Mama Marie had made sure he knew about the land of his fathers – both his natural father and Papa Bill – for both had come originally from this far northern county. He had never in his wildest dreams expected to see it, but now he had and he was glad. It was a good heritage.

He loved Canada and it was his home. The ranch that he had built up into a prosperous business there would support Hugo comfortably through his education. But there was something special about this lovely place of moorland and mountain wilderness, of small crofts scratching a living on thin soil, the endless sky – and in the summer, endless light. Caithness had got its hooks into his heart and Hugh knew he would never forget it.

At last, he rose and shouldered his pack. He thought about simply crossing the road and taking the swiftest way back to camp but he wanted to prolong his day. He decided he would scramble down the

211

hill and maybe take a look into the sawmill to see how the boys were doing.

As he pushed open the door, a voice greeted him, 'Hey, it's the Sarge!'

'What are you doing here?' another called. 'You should be off enjoying yourself!'

The stone building was full of the sweet sawdusty smell of newly cut wood. Hugh greeted the men, who were hard at work feeding lengths of larch into the Scotch table saw. Its huge jagged teeth made short work of even the toughest tree trunk and the men were getting up a fine speed.

They laughed and bantered in French and English as they worked.

'Regular cardsharp, the Sarge,' one of the men joked. 'I reckon you fixed that deck! I never win any prizes at the whist drives!'

'Neither do I usually,' Hugh said. 'Maybe my luck's turned!'

Quickly glancing round to make sure all was going well, he made his farewells and turned to leave. But just as he reached the door, a noise pulled him back.

A shout of alarm. A stumble. A man losing his balance. Too close to that lethal turning blade.

Hugh was there in an instant. He pulled the man clear, but the man was still off-balance. As he leaned in to hold the man safe, Hugh instinctively put out a hand to steady himself – and saw the fresh red blood fly as the saw teeth caught his hand and with a sickening noise, sliced through flesh, bone and sinew.

CHAPTER 61

'Bit drastic, wasn't it?'

An attractive young woman was standing in front of his chair, a cup of tea in her hands.

Her question stirred Hugh out of his apathy. He had been sitting beside his bed in the hospital ward, gazing into space and thinking dark thoughts. The whirling table saw had slashed into his right hand, severing most of his fingers, and now he was left with a useless fist instead of a hand. So much for his luck turning!

He would never be able to play cards again. And as for wielding an axe or firing a rifle… His days in the Forestry Corps were over. He would be sent home, wounded – but not gloriously in battle. Instead he would be invalided out by a stupid accident. And there was no glory or pride in that.

And what would he do once he got home? Before he had left Canada, he had set up the ranch and the accompanying businesses with good competent managers to run them. He had accountants to see to the books, other people to do everything that needed doing, including paying Hugo's school fees. Hugo was happily settled at his school, spending his holidays with his friends or at his grandmother's home. He didn't need his father any more. So, Hugh despaired, what was he going to do with the rest of his life – and with only one hand?

The girl with the teacup gestured to the bandages on what was left of Hugh's hand.

'So what happened?'

Hugh looked at her. There was no sympathy in her face, just blunt curiosity. He liked that.

'Sawmill,' he said shortly. 'My hand got in the way of the saw.'

Her eyes steadied on his face. 'Stupid, then?' she queried. 'Or were you wanting to go home?'

Hugh's eyes crinkled in a surprised grin. Few people – pretty girls especially – would have the nerve to state these things out loud, though they might indeed think them.

'Stupid,' he said shortly. 'What's your name?'

'Ruby,' the girl said. 'Ruby Cormack. Mrs.'

Hugh's eyes narrowed. Warning him off, was she? And suddenly the thought blossomed delightfully as new life surged into Hugh. If she was warning him off, then he was not finished yet – not if this lovely young woman thought he was fit enough to need warning off!

He grinned. 'Mrs?' he queried.

She extended her left hand to display a wedding ring and an engagement ring with a tiny diamond.

'I see,' Hugh said. 'That's a pity...'

Her mouth quivered with laughter. So she was flirting with him. Mmm, two could play that game.

'Your husband... is away fighting?' he queried.

He knew many young wives were willing to find diversion among home-based troops in their husbands' absence. He hoped that might be so in this case. He liked the look of this girl.

As he waited for the answer, Hugh realised he was holding his breath. And suddenly he felt like a schoolboy. He felt young and carefree for the first time in years. Perhaps there was life in the old dog yet… and a bit of fun to be had before he was shipped off home.

'No,' the girl said. 'No, he's not. Now, can you manage this cup of tea with your other hand?' She held it out to him.

Hugh took his time reaching for the cup. 'Yes,' he said. 'I can manage a lot of things with my other hand.' He grinned at her. 'I'm left-handed.'

Ruby's eyes twinkled appreciatively as she handed the cup of tea over to Hugh. She watched carefully as he handled it smoothly. He took a long, satisfying swallow of the tea, and looked up to find her eyes still on him.

'So you've got a husband at home,' he said. 'Lucky man. And I've got no one, just a ranch back in Canada and…'

'No,' Ruby interrupted. 'I've not got a husband waiting for me at home. I'm a widow. He was killed at St Valery in '40.'

She turned to go.

'Ruby!'

She turned back.

'My dear, I'm sorry…'

'Don't be,' she said shortly. 'There's a war on and these things happen.'

'True,' he said, holding up the bandaged stump of his hand. 'Things happen. But good things can maybe happen too.'

He held her gaze for a moment, watching her thinking, considering, then he lowered his lips to his teacup and drank his tea as she walked away.

CHAPTER 62

'You look mighty pleased with yourself,' George commented sourly.

He had arrived without warning to take delivery of another load of illicit whisky. He threw his chauffeur's cap down on the sideboard and crossed the room to take Ruby in his arms.

'Well, I couldn't say the same about you,' Ruby said. 'What's the matter? Is domestic bliss not agreeing with you?'

George took a step back, releasing her, his face suddenly filled with fury. For a moment Ruby feared she had gone too far, but he simply said 'Get me a whisky' and flung himself into an armchair.

Dutifully she fetched glass and bottle and poured him a generous shot. She watched him as he downed it, fast.

'So what's the problem?' she persisted. 'Home or business?'

'Business,' he said, holding out the glass for a refill. Duly replenished, he swirled the golden liquid round, gazing into the depths of the glass.

'Anything I can do to help?' she asked.

'I don't want to talk about it,' he grunted.

That bad, Ruby thought. She would find out in the end. She always did. She tried a sidetrack: 'I haven't seen you for a while.'

'Missed me?' His eyes glinted.

She took a deep breath. It had worked. Her lips curved in amusement. 'You're so vain! Why do you think I'd miss you?'

There was no way that Ruby would admit to the loneliness and heartache and anger she had felt these past weeks without a visit from George. She had understood he needed to repair his relations with the Cormacks, but she saw no reason why that should preclude their arrangement...

He reached up and touched her cheek with his finger.

'You missed me. Go on, admit it!'

Ruby laughed. 'No. I've been too busy.' She sauntered over to the other armchair and settled herself comfortably.

'Oh yes?' George queried suspiciously. 'And just exactly what has been keeping you busy?'

'Or who?' Ruby suggested daringly.

George's dark eyes flashed.

Ruby suppressed a grin. 'I've been busy at the hospital,' she said. 'Lots of new patients... And one or two interesting ones. Canadians,' she added with studied nonchalance. 'Men with big ranches back home. Men without wives.' She watched his reaction.

His eyes narrowed.

'Is that so?' he said slowly.

She smiled.

'Yes,' she said. 'That's so.'

'And how do they come to be in your hospital, these rich Canadians with their big ranches?' George's voice was silky.

'The Canadian Forestry Corps is based at Berriedale. They're cutting down the trees at Langwell,' Ruby said. She shrugged. 'Accidents happen – in the woods, at the sawmill...'

'And?'

217

'And if the accident is bad enough, they'll get sent back to Canada...'

'To their big ranches?'

She nodded.

'You could do worse,' George said. He set down his glass, stood up and stalked from the room. Ruby heard the front door slam.

Interesting. Had she managed to make him just a little jealous? Good. It would do no harm.

And in the meantime there was that Hugh Mackay for a little light entertainment. Though, Ruby considered, if George did not show more interest, Hugh could perhaps prove to be more than light entertainment.

After all, as George so rightly said, she could do worse...

CHAPTER 63

'I'm sure there's a perfectly acceptable reason,' Mr Cormack said, but his eyes said otherwise.

George looked at his father-in-law and considered the options open to him. He had not expected him to bother looking at the books for several months yet. It was the wrong time of year. The tax year ended in April. There was no need for him to go examining the books.

Unless something had alerted him to George's activities? But surely that could not be so? He had been very careful. In general he kept his illegal activities well separated from his respectable day-job. But sometimes there was a necessity – a little extra petrol off the ration-book to a friend helping with the illicit whisky-running, a little change from the till… Well, perhaps more than that. George had to admit he had got used to dipping into the funds from the cash drawer under the counter, especially now that he had persuaded Mr Cormack to let him take over the management of the business – including the finances.

Another heart attack had forced Rab Cormack to take life easier, and to delegate more. George had stepped in quickly to take up the reins.

'My stepfather made sure I knew how to run a business,' he had told Mr Cormack. 'The hacienda supplied top-quality beef to the meat-processing plant in Buenos Aires, then when he expanded the business with more land and more cattle, he needed another meat-processing plant so I was sent to Chicago to oversee the business side there.' He had spread his hands and shrugged. 'I am used to business affairs!'

The description of his stepfather's empire far outclassed the Cormack's business and Mr Cormack was duly impressed. Like his son Bobby, he had always been more interested in the motor cars themselves and the oily engines which lay in parts on the workshop floor. Now he could spend his days in the workshop tinkering with the motor cars, leaving the day-to-day business to George.

Which was exactly as George had planned. So what had now aroused Mr Cormack's curiosity?

Surely Joyce had nothing to complain of? He was the most attentive of husbands! So attentive that he feared he was no longer able to visit Ruby often enough for her liking. And with fewer visits, he had been forced to resort to providing expensive presents to keep her happy...

And suddenly George saw the problem. The latest gift... But how could he provide an explanation Mr Cormack might accept? George racked his brains, running through the possibilities. And yes. There was an answer. George arranged his features to display appropriate embarrassment, and held up a hand as though attempting to pacify the man.

'The new baby...'

Mr Cormack's eyes narrowed.

'Am I not paying you enough?'

'No, no,' George protested. 'The thing is I saw this beautiful ring and I thought how Joyce would love it. A gift for when the baby arrives. What do you call it…?' He searched his memory for the English word. 'An eternity ring, that's it. That's what it's called.'

Mr Cormack nodded, his face less threatening.

George continued. 'I confess it was on the black market – that was why I could not do hire-purchase.' He looked up. 'It is expensive.' He shrugged and raised his hands in mock defeat. 'But she deserves it, no?'

He waited for Mr Cormack to agree, then continued. 'I have borrowed the money. I'm sorry,' he said. 'It was only to be a temporary loan. I will pay it back. I assure you.' He drew himself up to his full height and flashed an indignant glare at Mr Cormack. 'I am no thief. And this was family money, no? To buy something special – it was an amazing opportunity – for your daughter, my wife.'

George held his breath. So long as Mr Cormack did not ask to see the ring… He had indeed bought a ring with some of the money he had taken from the business but he had given it to Ruby. If he really needed to, he might just be able to get it back…

Mr Cormack was shaking his head. George waited, trying for a penitent posture.

'Well, in that case,' Mr Cormack said slowly, 'I can understand. But see you pay it back and make sure it doesn't happen again. If you need money, you just come directly to me. You understand?'

His gaze was fierce but George drew a deep breath. He was in the clear.

The door from the street swung open and then the door into the office. Ruby, in smart street clothes, drew a man in Canadian Forestry Corps uniform into the room. She spotted George and smiled at him, then she drew the Canadian forward.

'Hugh, I'd like you to meet some more of my family,' she spoke to the Canadian. 'This is my father-in-law, Mr Cormack. He owns this garage and the hire cars, the ambulances, and the hearses. I used to work here before I was married.'

'Hugh Mackay,' Hugh introduced himself. He took his bandaged right hand out of his pocket. 'You'll forgive me if I don't shake hands, sir. I was recently injured – an accident at the sawmill.'

'He was trying to save one of the men from worse harm,' Ruby said. 'I met him at the hospital where I've been helping out.' She smiled sunnily in the face of George's sudden scowl. 'And this is my sister-in-law's husband...'

At that moment the house door opened and Mrs Cormack and a heavily pregnant Joyce entered.

'Rab, I was looking for you...' Mrs Cormack said. Smiling at the little group in the office, she said, 'Hello, Ruby, my dear. And who is this?'

'Hugh Mackay, ma'am,' Hugh said, coming forward. He gestured again to his bandaged hand. 'Please forgive me for not shaking hands...'

Hannah Cormack looked curiously at the man.

'And you're from where?'

'I'm from Canada, ma'am,' Hugh said. 'But my forebears came from hereabouts.'

'Ah yes, and who might they be?' Hannah asked with interest.

'My father was a Mackay, from south of Thrumster.'

Hannah's brow furrowed a moment as she took in the information, then she stared at Hugh as sudden enlightenment dawned.

'Hugh Mackay? After your father, of course. And he was Hughie Mackay...'

Hugh nodded.

'He went to the Klondike?' Hannah continued.

'That's him,' Hugh began.

'Hugh has given me the darlingest ring,' Ruby interrupted. 'It was made from some of the Klondike gold his father found!'

She held up her hand to show off the ring.

'Isn't it lovely?'

CHAPTER 64

'May I see?' Joyce asked, coming forward.

With a triumphant glance at George, Ruby held her hand out to Joyce.

'Please do.'

Joined by her mother, Joyce bent over the ring on Ruby's hand, tracing the shape of the ivy leaf that graced the front of the ring and the word, Mizpah, in raised letters on it.

'Oh, that is pretty!' she murmured.

And suddenly Hannah Cormack heard the echo of her own voice from many years past. With sudden clarity she remembered saying those words as she looked at the very same ring. She looked at it again, closely. Yes, she was sure. It was the same ring.

She remembered so clearly the young Hughie Mackay who had had the ring made out of Klondike gold. He had sent it home to her sister Belle to whom he was secretly engaged.

But Belle had broken off the engagement... when she heard from Hughie's friend and partner in the Klondike that Hughie was involved with a dance-hall girl out there, and the girl was pregnant.

'It was my mother's,' Hugh was saying. 'She gave it to me.'

So had Hughie given it to that girl, the dance-hall girl, Hannah wondered. Or was Hugh's mother someone else entirely?

'My father died before I was born,' Hugh continued. 'My mother went to my father's uncle and aunt in Manitoba and they looked after us. After they died, I inherited the ranch. They had no children of their own.'

Ah, Hannah thought, *that must mean that Hugh's mother was the dance-hall girl*. She hoped Hughie had had time to marry her before he died.

But no, wait. Wasn't he killed? Murdered by the very friend who had written home to Belle and spilled the beans about the dance-hall girl? What was that man's name? Hannah puzzled over her memories. It was all so very long ago.

Joyce was still admiring the ring.

'And it's made out of gold your father found in the Klondike?' she asked.

Hugh nodded.

'George darling,' Joyce said suddenly. 'Isn't that an amazing coincidence? Your father was in the Klondike too and he found gold.'

George smiled, a wide disparaging smile.

'Thousands of people poured into the Klondike during those years,' he said.

Hannah's head came up then and she scrutinised George's bland face. He had spoken the merest truth. The Gold Rush had seen tens of thousands of prospectors descend on the Klondike area. But Hannah knew there was more to this story. Because George's father had been in the Klondike too and his name was George St Clair. The Wick version rang loud and horribly clear in Hannah's memory: Geordie Sinclair. And that Geordie Sinclair had gone to the Klondike with young Hughie Mackay. And it was he who had written in bitter jealousy to her sister Belle. And he who, if the story that eventually came back was true, had killed Hughie Mackay.

Hannah looked from George to Hugh. She remembered young Hughie Mackay and now she could see a likeness in his son. The same gentle good looks and easy-going nature. And she well remembered the scoundrel that had been Geordie Sinclair.

So this George St Clair was his son. And her beloved only daughter was married to him. Shaken, she struggled to follow the continuing conversation.

Joyce was tracing the word written in raised letters across the centre of the ivy leaf that adorned the ring.

'Mizpah,' she said in a questioning tone.

'It's from the Bible,' Hannah found herself saying, remembering her own mother's explanation all those years ago. 'It means "May the Lord watch between me and thee, while we are absent from one another." That's what it means.'

'That's lovely,' Joyce said, then added, 'Oh, of course. You'll be going back to Canada?'

She gestured to Hugh's injured hand. No longer able-bodied and able to work or fight, he would surely be demobbed and sent home.

But Hugh smiled, his eyes on Ruby.

'I'm not sure about that,' he said. 'I've been thinking. I like it over here. The ranch – my business – is in safe hands while I'm away. I've no need to rush back.'

Ruby smiled and Hugh's gaze ranged amiably over the people around him.

'If I can find something to do with myself – some useful work – I might just stay a while.'

CHAPTER 65

Hannah watched the young folk as they chatted cheerfully. She noted that from time to time, George threw a watchful glance at her. She schooled herself to remain calm and smiling, gently interested in their conversation, but she longed to get away and think.

What could she do? What could they do? It felt like a nightmare. Here, after all these years, in one place, were the sons of Geordie Sinclair and Hughie Mackay. And it seemed they had no idea of the terrible connection between them. Hannah longed to pour it all out to Rab, but his health was so poor, his heart might not be up to a shock of this magnitude.

At last, Ruby and Hugh took their leave and Joyce announced her intention of going home. Mindful of George's implacable dark eyes on her, Hannah kissed her daughter and opened the door back to the house. As she stepped through, it felt like sanctuary.

But there was only one sanctuary, one refuge that was up to this situation. Hannah went through to the sitting room and reached for her Bible. She settled down by the fire and tried to order her thoughts. Stroking the familiar old leather cover was soothing.

She wondered suddenly what happened to the Bible Hughie's mother had given him when he left on the train for his fateful journey to the Klondike. She remembered Geordie Sinclair's dark mocking presence beside him on the train that morning.

She had been sure Belle was at the root of all the trouble. Belle who had wanted the life of a lady, money, a fine house, fine clothes, and a rich handsome husband dancing attendance on her every whim. Beautiful Belle. It was not surprising all the young men in town had been in love with her. And it was not surprising when that ne'er-do-well Geordie Sinclair tried his luck and proposed to her that Belle turned him down smartish. Belle had a sharp tongue and her rejection had clearly rankled.

And then poor young Hughie got caught in her toils and nothing would do but for him to seek his fortune in the Klondike so he could be the rich man Belle desired. Hannah had to concede that a poor crofter's son would not have won her father's approval either.

Somehow Belle had persuaded Hughie – he was such an innocent! – to enter a secret engagement with her, and when he found gold he had sent the Mizpah ring as her engagement ring.

Somehow Geordie had found a way to accompany Hughie to the Klondike, no doubt exploiting the lad's good nature and innocence. And then when gold was found, Hughie had spent some of it on a dance-hall girl who had got pregnant. Geordie had seized his chance and written to Belle, getting his revenge for her rejection.

Hannah remembered Belle's fury. The Mizpah ring she had worn on a chain under her blouse vanished – sent back to Canada – and the secret engagement – secret no more – was ended. Belle was sent to an aunt's in Edinburgh till the scandal died down. She went to work at a fine tailoring establishment. And Belle, being Belle, cast her eyes – and her lures – on Adam Finlayson, the heir to the business.

Hannah sighed. Rab had provided the next instalment of the story – that strange encounter with Adam during the war had brought all those secrets out into the open. He had told her all when he came home and she had been so grateful for the second chance God had given them.

But now! Now what were they going to do? It was as if the wheel had turned and now the next generation were entangled in the terrible web of deceit and hurt that Belle had so unwittingly unleashed all those years ago.

Her beloved daughter, Joyce – named for the joy of her reunion with Rab – was married to the son of that scoundrel Geordie Sinclair. And if she was not much mistaken he was a chip off the old block. A scoundrel in his own right. She remembered the bruises on Joyce's face. Her flinching fear. Despite her daughter's protestations, she was not convinced that theirs was a happy marriage. She could not believe that all was as it should be.

And now there was Hugh Mackay. So like his father. Innocent, easy-going – and maybe easily led. Was Ruby looking on him as her meal-ticket to a better life, as maybe she had with Bobby? Hannah took herself to task. Was it any of her business?

But she would always see Hughie as Belle's victim. If Belle had not played her wicked games with him he might still be alive, well, happily married with a family of his own at home in Caithness – like her beloved Rab.

Suddenly, Hannah was clear in her own mind. She did not want Hughie's son damaged or destroyed. Not if she could help it.

He needed a job and he needed somewhere to stay after he was demobbed. Surely they could help? They could find work for him. He said he was left-handed. And there was room for him here in the house.

That way at least she could keep an eye on him. And on Ruby. And George. And her daughter.

She would watch and wait and do whatever she could.

'In Your strength, Lord,' Hannah prayed as she laid it all before her Lord. 'Your will be done.'

CHAPTER 66

'It's time I was going,' Ruby said. 'I don't want to miss the bus home.' She smiled at Hugh. 'Thank you for the tea.'

'You're welcome,' Hugh said as he stood and helped her on with her coat, then accompanied her from the tearoom.

'How are you finding life with the Cormacks?' Ruby asked as they walked together to the bus stop.

'They're very kind,' Hugh said. 'To make room for me when they've already got two airmen billeted on them. I think it's marvellous.'

'Well, you're helping them out too,' Ruby pointed out.

'I'm enjoying it,' Hugh told her. 'It's good to feel useful again.' He gestured at his injured hand. 'I'm grateful to them not just for the room but for the job.'

'Being left-handed has come in handy,' Ruby said. 'Anyone else – anyone right-handed – would have been in real trouble.'

'That's right,' Hugh agreed. 'I need to count my blessings!'

'So how are things at work?' Ruby asked curiously.

'George and I are getting on really well,' Hugh said. 'We make a good team. He does the hires; I see to the business side. And it takes all the weight off Mr Cormack's shoulders. He's not been at all well these past few weeks.'

'He's not getting any younger,' Ruby agreed.

'No. I think it's really too much for him now,' Hugh said. His steps slowed to a halt and Ruby turned to look at him. 'Ruby, I've been thinking...'

She held his gaze, hardly daring to breathe. Was he going to propose to her at last? It was what she had been working towards since the first day she met him at the hospital. She knew giving her the Mizpah ring had been a gesture of friendship, maybe even of promise, but she was still waiting for his proposal. With his ranch in Canada and all the other businesses, he was a good catch for a girl like her.

'I like it here,' Hugh was saying.

Ruby nodded, but her mind was racing. What was he thinking? Shouldn't he be proposing marriage and then a rapid trip back to Canada for the pair of them, away from all this war and the shortages and the beastly rationing?

'I'm thinking I'd like to stay here. If you'll have me?' He paused, searching her eyes. 'Mr Cormack wants to give up the business. I've been speaking to George.'

Ruby's eyes narrowed. That was not a good sign. George would always steer Hugh towards whatever would benefit George most. Though to be fair, that usually meant it would benefit Ruby too. She waited to hear what Hugh would say.

'I'm thinking of selling up in Canada and putting my money into the business here,' Hugh continued. 'Then George and I will be partners. We will run it together...' He paused. 'Ruby,' Hugh said earnestly. 'What do you say?'

'I'm not sure, my dear,' she said.

She had assumed that Hugh working in the office at the garage was a temporary thing, just till the end of the war, then they would start a new life together in Canada. But if he were to sell up the ranch…

'I know I'm not much use with this hand…' Hugh was saying.

'It's not that,' Ruby told him. 'I just need to think about it.'

'I thought you liked me…'

'Oh, I do,' Ruby assured him.

But would he be easier to like away from George in Canada, or here, with his money invested in the garage in Wick?

She needed to talk to George. She needed to know exactly where this idea of Hugh's fitted into his plans – and how she would fit into them if she were Hugh's wife.

CHAPTER 67

1944

'I know what I'm doing,' George said when Ruby finally cornered him and asked him. 'Just trust me. This will be very much to your advantage as well as mine.'

So Ruby married Hugh. He sold the ranch and his other businesses, invested the money in a buy-out of the garage business which he now co-owned with George and, in a surprising move, brought his teenage son to Britain.

They had gone down to Gourock to welcome the boy from the ship that had brought him from Canada. At the dockside Ruby had scoured the clusters of disembarking passengers for a youngster, but it was a tall young man with unfriendly eyes who came towards them.

Hugh had enfolded him in a warm embrace and there had been a bit of fussing from the boy about Hugh's now perfectly healed injury. Then Hugh had turned the lad towards her.

'Meet your new mama!' Hugh had introduced her enthusiastically as if there could be any doubt. The old Mizpah ring sat on her finger alongside a shiny new wedding ring.

Hugo had given her what could only be described as an appraising look. Ruby, who had planned to bestow warm motherly kisses on a biddable stepson, found herself at a loss. It appeared that Hugh's plan for a happy family was meeting with no encouragement from his son.

Determinedly she stepped forward and placed a kiss on the cold cheek.

'Welcome to Scotland,' she said.

She had managed to maintain some silly chatter as they loaded Hugo's luggage into the big car and set off for home, but her mind was racing. There was no room for this hostile young man in the life she had so carefully built for herself. And he seemed alarmingly intelligent. If she was not careful, a sharp-eyed Hugo might just cotton on to what was really going on behind the scenes with her and George – both their relationship and their other business activities.

By the time they reached home, it was clear that all Ruby's efforts at making friends with her stepson had failed. He appeared to be the one male she would not be able to charm. The couple of weeks' holiday before he was due to start school were going to be a nightmare.

But she had reckoned without her daughter. At all of four years of age, Amanda was a shocking flirt and she soon had Hugo wound around her little finger. And when the heavily pregnant Joyce came to visit, bringing three-year-old Georgie, it was obvious that Hugo had hidden Pied Piper talents because the two little ones adored him and followed him around everywhere.

'No, ma'am, they're no trouble,' he had declared when Joyce had apologised. 'I don't have any brothers or sisters, so it's a new experience for me!'

'He's a nice boy,' Joyce had said to Ruby afterwards. 'You're so lucky!'

'But what am I going to do?' Ruby had asked George. 'He doesn't like me. He doesn't like Scotland. He hates his dad being married again. The atmosphere at home you could cut with a knife. It's bad enough having to keep Hugh sweet...'

'Leave it with me,' was all George had said and when the time came for Hugo to enrol at the local High School, Ruby discovered there had been a change of plan. Hugo was to go to a private school in Edinburgh.

Even the usually non-interventionist Mrs Cormack had queried the plan.

'But why?' she asked. 'The High School is excellent. As good a school as can be.'

'Yes, I'm sure,' Hugh had said defensively. 'But my boy is bright and he deserves a first-class education – the best money can buy.'

Mrs Cormack had frowned then. 'Well, maybe that's how it is in Canada, but that's not what it's like in Scotland. In Scotland everybody gets the best education – and what they make of it is up to them.'

'Well, my boy is clever,' Hugh had declared, 'and he deserves the best. So it's Edinburgh and boarding school for him now, and after school, he will go to Edinburgh University!'

Good, Ruby thought. By the time he finished university, they would be well settled in their marriage and he could not cause any harm. She would surely manage to cope with him in the holidays!

And so Hugo had been waved goodbye at the railway station, the little girls excited by the outing and waving delightedly. Ruby had returned home with a lighter heart. She could get back to enjoying her life.

Their new house was a delight. It was one of the modern chalet bungalows in West Banks Avenue, with a pretty garden in front and plenty of ground behind that Hugh was having turned into a productive vegetable garden.

Ruby stood on the doorstep and pulled on her brand-new expensive leather gloves. She patted her newly waved and styled hair. Yes, everything was going beautifully.

According to plan. George's plan.

CHAPTER 68

1945

'What would you like for your tea tonight?' Hannah Cormack asked the two little girls who had followed her into the kitchenette at the back of the house. She reached inside one of the cupboards and took out two wooden egg-cups, painted a bright red. She held them up to the girls.

'What about a nice brown boiled egg and soldiers? Would you like that?'

Five-year-old Amanda pouted her displeasure, but her younger cousin, Georgie, nodded, her silky dark hair bobbing against her cheeks.

'Yes, please, Granny,' she said politely.

'Amanda?' Hannah gently queried.

The little girl tossed her head. 'I suppose so,' she said ungraciously.

'Then that's what you'll have.' She pointed to the chairs set beside the kitchen table. 'Sit down there at the table, girls, and I'll see to your tea.'

Obediently four-year-old Georgie started to climb up onto the nearest chair but Amanda pushed her away.

'That's my chair!' she said. 'You have to have another one.'

Triumphantly she sat herself on the chair and watched Georgie go round the table and climb up on another seat.

'Now, now, Amanda,' Hannah said disapprovingly. 'That's not nice. And this is not your house so these are not your chairs.'

Amanda glowered but Georgie was looking puzzled.

'Granny?' she asked.

'Yes, my dear?'

'How long will Mummy be away?'

Hannah Cormack paused in her work and glanced up at the clock on the kitchen mantlepiece. Joyce had gone into labour in the early hours of the morning and it was now four o'clock.

'I don't know, darling. Babies take as much time to arrive as they need. It varies. Sometimes a long time, sometimes not. We'll just have to wait and see.'

She popped two eggs into the water in the saucepan and placed the pan on the hot stovetop.

'Don't you worry,' she encouraged her. 'You'll be fine here with me and Amanda, and before you know it, you'll have a little brother or sister to play with.'

'I'd like a brother,' Georgie said seriously. 'I don't need a sister. I've got Amanda.'

Her grandmother turned quickly, but the child's face was blandly innocent of the hidden truth she had unknowingly voiced. Surely she did not know? Hannah was almost certain Joyce did not suspect. But she was convinced – as sure as sure could be – that Amanda was George's daughter. Seeing the two little girls together, as they sat at the kitchen table, the likeness was uncanny.

What was surprising was that no one had yet commented on it. In a small town like Wick, any possibility for gossip was usually seized on with glee. But then Amanda was supposed to be Bobby's daughter, and Bobby was Joyce's half-brother – and they were both Rab's children, so at a pinch...

But it was quite a pinch.

The water in the saucepan began to bubble and Hannah had to focus her attention on timing the eggs perfectly for her granddaughters. She had to admit that of the two, it was Georgie who held her heart.

George's daughter she might be, but she loved her dearly. That man... and his father. How she hoped little Georgie would not carry their bad blood. She feared for Amanda already. Her sulks and self-centredness did not bode well for the future.

Poor young Hughie Mackay had been gullible, easily led... just like his son, now neatly entrapped in marriage by a very smug Ruby. And his money funnelled into the garage by George St Clair. And maybe *his* son, young Hugo, was just as easily led. He was completely at the beck and call of the two little girls – especially that young madam, Amanda.

Hannah paused, gazing unseeing at the eggs in the boiling water. How grateful she was that her beloved Rab had not lived to see it all. And especially that she had never found the courage to tell him just who George and Hugh really were. His sudden death from a massive heart attack one day while he had been out in the garage doing something incomprehensible with a car engine had been a terrible shock. Every day she missed him. Every day she listened for his footstep...

'Granny! Are the eggs ready? I'm hungry!'

Amanda's insistent voice pulled Hannah back to what she was meant to be doing. She popped the now perfectly-timed eggs into their red egg-cups, set them on saucers with a spoon beside each and brought them to the table. The toast was ready too, so she quickly buttered it and cut it into strips, lining them up on the plates for the girls. Then she leaned over and swiftly and cleanly sliced the top off each egg.

'There!' she said. 'Will that do?'

'Yes, thank you, Granny,' Georgie said and set to with delight. Amanda simply fell to without a word.

Hannah pulled out a chair and sat with them to keep the children company. When Ruby had heard that Georgie would be staying with Hannah while Joyce was in the Henderson Memorial Nursing Home giving birth, she had simply turned up and deposited Amanda. Like a parcel. Or an unwanted puppy.

Hannah wondered just how much love there was for Amanda? Dear Bobby would surely have accepted the child as his own – if he had lived. And he would have loved her. That was his nature. Hugh did his best, but Ruby did not seem to have much of a maternal instinct.

'Company for Georgie!' Ruby had said gaily and taken herself off before Hannah could protest – or agree.

She looked at the two children sitting at her table. They had all been innocent children once, she thought. Rab, Hughie, Geordie, herself, Belle... Or perhaps not. She remembered another kitchen and her sister Belle having one of her tantrums. Belle had always wanted her own way – regardless of the cost to others.

Hannah remembered Belle's spiteful dying words. 'You'll never have him!' She turned the well-worn wedding ring on her finger. Well, Belle had been wrong. Everything had worked out well for them. She and Rab had shared more than forty years together. And they had been good years. Happy years.

Before that George St Clair turned up and spoiled everything. How could Joyce have made such a mistake? Surely they had brought her up in the knowledge of God and His Word? True, she was not the first girl from good Christian parents to find herself pregnant before her wedding day.

Hannah thought back. There had been something in George's demeanour, something calculating. She had always thought he had known exactly what he was doing – coming to the garage, befriending Bobby, getting a job, wheedling his way in… He was a good driver, she had to give him that. And when Bobby had been killed, he had very usefully filled that gaping hole. Rab would not have been able to continue running the business without him.

But Joyce had not been happy. Hannah remembered that bruise. She was sure that George had hit her daughter more than once. But Joyce had been adamant. She was determined to hang on to her marriage and George.

And then, of course, there was Ruby. Hannah had always wondered. Had Ruby been George's mistress from the start?

Hannah sighed. That brought them back to Amanda. She was sure Amanda was George's daughter.

And now today, or tomorrow, there would be another child of his getting. It was true George did seem to have changed his ways this last while. Was it possible for a man like him – a man of his blood and background – to change?

But surely everyone had a chance, whatever the start they had in life, to choose a different way? Or if they had initially gone wrong, to change and go right? Perhaps this was George's chance? Perhaps everything would turn out all right. Oh, she hoped everything would be all right.

Silently, she prayed: *Dear Lord, Your hand is on my family, I know that. Be with Joyce as she gives birth. Bring her through this safely. Bring our family through this, I pray. Amen.*

CHAPTER 69

George seized the telephone from Hugh.

'Yes?'

'It's a boy, Mr St Clair. Your wife has given birth to a boy.'

George let out a war whoop that rattled the glass on the office partition. Hugh, watching him closely, got up from his desk and slapped him on the back. Though George responded with a grin, he was still focusing on whatever was being said to him. Hugh returned to his desk and waited.

George's brow furrowed in puzzlement as he listened. Then he shrugged and replied, 'If I must. Whatever you say,' and put the telephone down.

'Congratulations,' Hugh said, standing up again. 'Shall we go and wet the baby's head?'

George grinned. 'Soon, my friend. Soon. I've got to go to the Nursing Home. I don't understand why. I suppose Joyce wants to see me. Tell you what, I'll meet you at the hotel in Watten, yes? We'll make a night of it!'

He laughed, jauntily threw on his hat and coat, and sauntered out.

~

'This way, Mr St Clair.'

The nurse led George upstairs and across the hallway of the gracious old house that had been turned into a maternity home several years before. She pushed open the door. There, sitting up in bed with a closely swaddled infant in her arms, was Joyce. She looked up and to his surprise, George saw sudden terror in her eyes.

'George,' she said, clutching the baby close to her.

'Thank you.' George dismissed the nurse and closed the door firmly behind her. He turned back to the bed. Why was Joyce behaving like this? Surely Joyce had not been unfaithful to him and the child bore the evidence only too clearly? But no. He knew exactly when the child had been conceived.

Could it be that the violence of the rape had done some damage to the child? No. That was not possible. So what was the problem? Some female nonsense...

'Well, my dear,' he said, tossing his hat onto the chair by the bed and moving towards her. 'Let me see my son and heir then.'

But Joyce held on to the child, protectively turned against her breast so George could not see his face.

'Joyce,' George said impatiently. 'I do not have time for games. I was asked to come. I have come. Let me see the child and then I will go.'

She swallowed hard and laid her head protectively over the child's, clearly unwilling to cooperate.

George reached out for the shawl-wrapped bundle.

'Let me see,' he said.

'George,' she pleaded, but he reached down and at last was able to prise the infant out of her grasp.

He looked down at the sleeping face, and sudden awareness took hold. And with it shock and rage. The child – his son! – the child he had pinned everything on… He struggled to find the words. The child was…

He thrust the infant back at Joyce.

'You stupid woman!' he shouted at her. 'Can't you do anything right? I needed a son to inherit the business – not this!' He pointed at the child in her arms. 'This creature! What good to me is this…' He stumbled, searching for the word in English.

Joyce burst into noisy tears, huddling into the bed, her arms surrounding the child, protecting him as best she could while George towered over her in his fury.

'Mr St Clair!' Matron's voice was firmly disapproving. He had not heard her come in. 'I know this has come as a shock…'

'And what do you know about it?' George said roughly as he pushed past her. 'What do any of you know?'

CHAPTER 70

George took the stairs two at a time and raced to the big black car, turning it with a loud crunching of gravel down the long drive and out into the main street. Fury consumed him. They had all let him down. Every one of them! Well, he was not finished yet.

He parked the car outside the office and ran in, pleased to see the place was empty. Hugh had clearly given everyone the rest of the day off and gone, as planned, to Watten.

George rifled the cash drawer under the counter, pocketing what he found there. Striding to Hugh's desk, he opened up the big cheque book and quickly wrote out a cheque.

As he wrote, he kept an ear on the house next door – children's voices: Georgie and Amanda. He stuffed the cheque in his pocket and headed back to the car. First the bank, then the house in Kinnaird Street for a few things…

Car packed, he drove quickly to West Banks. Ruby was just coming out of the bungalow. Quickly George leapt out of the car and seized her arm.

'Get your things,' he instructed her harshly. 'We're leaving. Now.'

'Leaving? What do you mean?' Ruby stared at George in astonishment.

'Don't ask questions,' he snapped. 'Either you come with me now or you stay here. It's up to you. But I'm leaving here. Today. Now.'

Ruby searched George's face. Angry but determined, he stared back.

'I've had enough of this place,' he said. 'Nothing's working. It's all gone wrong. I've had enough. It's time to cut loose, start again. I'm going back to Glasgow – for a start. Then maybe America, or Argentina. Now this stupid war is over, we can go anywhere. I'll decide later.'

The exciting names rang in Ruby's ears. Going places with George – being with George – that was all she had wanted. She paused.

'But what about Joyce... and the new baby?'

As she spoke she saw the answer in George's face.

'She couldn't even get that right!' he snarled.

'Another girl?'

'No!' George dismissed the idea. 'That would have been bad enough, but... What do you call it?' He pronounced the word with a Spanish accent: 'Mongol.'

Ruby's eyes widened. 'Oh George, I am sorry!'

George waved that away. 'Are you coming?' he demanded. 'It's up to you. But I'm going...'

'Yes,' Ruby said, 'I'm coming with you. Give me a minute,' and hurried into the house to pack. Her heart sang. They were going away – together! They would make a fresh start somewhere else, somewhere exciting! She couldn't wait!

As she threw some clothes into a suitcase, she reached for her make-up and perfume from the dressing-table and caught sight of the rings on her left hand. She slipped off the wedding ring, then the Mizpah ring. That tawdry old thing! She laughed. Surely George would buy her better jewellery than these. She left them lying on the dressing table.

As she closed the front door behind her, she had a sudden thought.

'What about Amanda? She's at Mrs Cormack's.'

'She'll be all right. Mrs Cormack will look after her,' George said carelessly as he helped Ruby into the car. 'We don't need a kid slowing us down.'

'True,' Ruby said. 'We'll be better off, just the two of ourselves.'

She settled down into the passenger seat, exchanging a triumphant grin with George. He switched on the engine and pointed the big black car south out of Wick.

~

The rain began as they left Latheron. Dark clouds shadowed the road, and slashes of lightning made Ruby jump. George was driving as though all the demons of hell were behind him.

'Are you going to tell me why we're leaving in such a rush?' she asked.

'I told you. I've had enough,' he ground out, swinging the car roughly round a tight bend.

Ruby caught her breath and held on tight.

'A clever man knows when to cut his losses,' George said, 'and now is the time for me.'

Another savage manoeuvre. The tyres squealed in protest but George forced the car on. He reached into his pocket and pulled out a fistful of banknotes. 'But I didn't leave empty-handed!' He laughed. 'I've cleaned the business out!'

'Oh George!' Ruby exclaimed, grabbing the notes from him. 'Is that why we're in such a hurry? So we get away before they notice...'

'That's right,' he said. 'We'll be long gone before they realise...'

Another sudden peal of thunder shook the heavens and the rain began to drum on the windscreen and the roof of the car.

'We'll be in Glasgow tonight,' he said. 'We're on our way out of here!'

'Oh George!' Ruby cried in delight, but as the car swung round the first sharp bend at the top of Berriedale hill, her voice rose in sudden panic.

'George!' she cried as he wrenched the wheel, trying to correct the slew of tyres sliding out of control on the wet road.

Her scream died as the car crashed through the dry-stone wall that edged the road and into the steepness of the field beyond, before plunging headlong towards the jagged rocks and the sea beneath.

CHAPTER 71

'George has gone?'

Joyce stared at her mother as she tried to take in what she was saying.

'*Gone?*' Joyce repeated the word.

She cradled her son gently in her arms, smiling softly at him, then looked up at her mother over the baby's sleeping face.

'I'm sorry, my dear,' Hannah Cormack said. 'I know you loved him...'

'I did for a while,' Joyce mused. 'At the beginning. Well, I thought I did. And I tried to, later, when he seemed to be trying... But now...' She looked down at her sleeping son. 'Now, I don't really think I ever did.' She caressed the baby's cheek. 'This one matters much more...'

She looked up at her mother. 'So if he's gone, I don't really mind. I should imagine you're thinking "Good riddance!"' She smiled. 'And maybe I am too.'

She paused, thoughtfully, then added quietly, 'Has he gone on his own, or has he taken Ruby with him?'

She saw the answer in her mother's eyes.

'Hugh will be so hurt,' Joyce said. 'Poor Hugh. I think he loved

Ruby. Funny how they all loved Ruby – Bobby, Hugh, maybe even George...'

Hannah wondered at her daughter's reaction. So she had known more of what had been going on than she had realised. Maybe she underestimated Joyce. But there was one thing she had to clarify.

'Joyce, my love, when I said George had gone, I meant...' She took a deep breath and looked up to find Joyce's dark eyes fixed steadily on her. 'George has gone for ever. He's dead. There was an accident. At Berriedale. He must have been taking that first bend too fast or too wide in the rain, and the car went over the clifftop.'

They both knew how dangerous Berriedale Braes were, even for an experienced and careful driver. And below the first bend was a steep rocky drop to the shore below.

'Dead?' Joyce echoed.

'Yes,' her mother said. She swallowed hard and added, 'And Ruby too.'

'Oh,' Joyce said. Her eyes filled with tears. 'How very sad. How very, very sad.'

Hannah gazed at her daughter in surprise. That she could find it in her heart, even now, to have compassion on the man who had treated her so badly, and the woman who had been his partner in wickedness... Yes, Hannah thought. She had underestimated her daughter. Or... or perhaps what Joyce had suffered at their hands had blossomed into maturity and strength and true beauty.

Thank You, Lord, Hannah prayed silently. *Please bring real good out of this...*

'What about Amanda?' Joyce was asking.

'She's with me. She'll be company for Georgie for the next few days till we sort out where she should go. I shouldn't think Hugh is in any state to cope with her. I'm sure Ruby's mother in Lybster would have her.'

'Yes,' Joyce said. 'That would probably be best.'

The baby began to grizzle and Joyce rocked him tenderly.

'Joyce, about the baby...' her mother began.

Joyce's eyes flashed a sudden warning.

'He's my son and he's a lovely baby,' she said. 'I'll hear nothing against him.' She glared at her mother. 'And I'll be bringing him home like any other baby and I'll be bringing him up like any other baby...' She faltered.

'My dear, that bit may not be true and you know that,' her mother corrected her gently. 'He will need more care and attention. His health...'

Joyce's chin came up defiantly. 'I don't care. He's my baby and we'll manage – between us.' She bent and placed a kiss on the baby's brow. 'And he'll have as good a life as he can for as long as he has it. And who his father was and how he came into the world and what the world thinks is the matter with him – none of that matters to me. I'm his mother and I love him.'

Hannah leaned over and kissed her daughter and her grandson, tears in her eyes

'And I'm his grandmother and I love him, just as I love you. We'll manage,' she said. 'Between us – and the good Lord – we'll manage.'

CHAPTER 72

'Dad?'

Hugh Mackay turned from his desk to look with surprise at the young man who had quietly entered the office.

'What are you doing here? You should be at school.'

'I couldn't stay there,' Hugo said. 'I know you want me to have a good education – but to think of you all alone up here... I just couldn't do it. I asked for compassionate leave.' He moved closer to his father. 'I'd like to stay for a while. I'd like to do what I can to help...'

Hugh stood up and flung his good arm round his son's shoulders. 'You're a good lad,' he said gruffly.

He threw himself back into his chair and gestured at the papers that littered the desk's surface. 'Though I don't know if anybody can help!'

Hugo pulled up a chair. 'Tell me,' he said and set himself to listen.

'So there's virtually nothing left,' his father concluded. 'George ran the business into the ground. All that's left is what he couldn't sell or take with him. It was a partnership and either of us could sign cheques. He cleared out the bank account before he went. Took it in cash.' Hugh sighed deeply. 'When they found the wreck of the car, there were a few banknotes fluttering around on the shore but that was all. The rest had all blown away!'

He ran his hand over his head. 'All I have left is the house. I could mortgage that but is it worth it?' He looked at Hugo. 'Do you want this business when I'm gone? If you do, I'll do everything I can to rescue it – but at the moment it looks like an impossible task.'

'Don't think like that,' Hugo told him. 'You're not going anywhere for a while yet! You need to be thinking about what *you* want to do!'

'Me? I'm tired,' Hugh said. 'Tired of it all! Look at me!' He waved the damaged right hand at Hugo. 'I came across here because I'd messed up in Canada and I was restless.' He laughed bitterly. 'I'd have been far better staying put.' He rose heavily to his feet. 'Come on. There's nothing more I can do here.'

As he reached for his coat and hat, the telephone rang.

'I'll just get that,' he said. 'Might be some good business coming our way.'

He picked up the telephone. 'Hugh Mackay here. How may I help you?'

Hugo smiled. He loved his father's old-fashioned courtesy.

'I'm sorry,' Hugh was saying now. 'I didn't quite catch that.'

Hugo could hear the muffled voice on the other end of the line.

'But...' Hugh said. 'But I thought...' He listened, then, 'Thank you. Yes. I understand. The day after tomorrow. I see. Thank you. Goodbye.'

He sat down heavily.

'Dad?'

His father looked up, his eyes dead and defeated.

'When I said all that's left was what George couldn't take with him, I was wrong. That was the solicitor. George sold everything...

The house, the office, the garage, the workshop, the cars…' As he enumerated each item, his face grew drawn and grey and his lips purpled. 'They've given me till the day after tomorrow to vacate the premises. And the house.'

'Dad!' Hugo protested. 'Don't go torturing yourself like this! We'll find a way! We'll come around…'

'We were partners,' Hugh was saying. 'Me and George… The kind of partnership where you need to trust somebody. But he sold it all over my head – and now there's…' He gasped, his good hand coming round to clutch at his chest.

'Dad!' Hugo stood up alarmed.

'Now, there's nothing…' Hugh's face twisted in pain. 'There's nothing left.' As his eyes glazed, he managed to force out the words 'Son, I am so sorry.'

CHAPTER 73

Georgie sat quiet as a mouse on the second step from the bottom of the stairs so she could hear what Mummy and Granny were saying in the kitchen. She hugged herself to keep warm. It was quite chilly out on the dark wooden stairs that coiled up and up to the top of the big old house. She was not sure that she liked it, not like their old house in Kinnaird Street or Granny's house. At night it was scary and dark and she ran up the stairs to her bedroom breathing prayers to protect her from the frightening shadows.

She shivered, but she knew if she put her nose inside the kitchen she would be sent away to play. Whatever was going on, they would not speak about it in front of her. She sighed. There had been a lot of that lately. Since Daddy died. And Amanda's mum. And Hugo's father.

Everything had changed. They had all moved house – even Granny. Now Granny was living with them – or were they living with her? Georgie was not sure. Whichever way it was, now they were all in this one house in Willowbank: Mum and the new baby, Granny, and Georgie.

She liked her new room tucked away at the very top of the house. It had the sweetest little fireplace and a window that stuck out of the roof and looked out over the bay and the harbour. Georgie loved to stand there and watch the boats and the lorries and the people. It was the best view in the whole world, especially when the moon came out and made magic white pathways across the sea.

And the people she loved the most in the whole world – well, most of them – were here too. Mum and her new baby brother Robbie were in the big front bedroom downstairs, and Granny had the pretty back bedroom next to the bathroom.

And there was a lovely long garden to play in. When the weather was better. Not like today when it was cold and wet and horrid.

The doorbell rang, suddenly loud in the echoing silence. Georgie jumped to her feet and scurried up a few steps to where the staircase took a sharp turn and she could be hidden from view. She peeked through the bannisters.

Granny had opened the door and was welcoming two ladies into the house. Georgie had never seen them before. They looked very alike in dark fur coats closed right up to the throat and hats that all but covered their faces, but once they had taken them off and given them to Granny, Georgie could see that they were very different. One was a youngish lady with lots of dark hair, a quite dark skin and flashing eyes. She spoke in a foreign accent. The other was an older lady more Granny's age, her hair silvery grey. Her voice was soft and gentle and her face looked sad.

Granny opened the sitting-room door and ushered them in. Georgie heard her say 'I'm sure you'd like a cup of tea to warm you up. You've had a long journey. And a sad one.'

Her mother came through now and there was handshaking and hugging and quite a lot of talking. Georgie watched Granny take the fur coats and hats through to the kitchen and a little later bring back a tray of tea. She noticed Granny had set out the best china and the big silver teapot so these must be special visitors.

She crept downstairs and into the kitchen. The fur coats were piled on a chair. Georgie could smell the damp fur. She reached out to touch and then leaned in to smell them, to feel the wet fur against her face. It was so soft and smelled dark and rich and musky.

'Georgie?' Granny had returned quietly.

'I was just…' Georgie pulled herself out of the soft cocoon of damp fur.

'It's all right, love,' her grandmother smiled. 'It's not every day we have such interesting visitors.'

'Who are they?'

'Come and meet them,' Granny invited her, and drew Georgie through to the sitting room where the ladies exclaimed with obvious delight.

Standing on the rug in front of the settee where the two ladies sat, Georgie examined them as curiously as they seemed to be examining her.

'This is your Aunt Catalena,' her grandmother introduced her to the dark-haired younger lady. 'She has come all the way from Buenos Aires in Argentina.'

Georgie's eyes grew round. That was where her father had come from.

'I had to come,' Catalena said. Dark sorrowful eyes roamed round the room, snagging Joyce's gaze. 'Jorge was my brother.' She shrugged. 'Half-brother, but no matter. When I was this one's age, I adored him. So I felt it should be me that should come.' She sighed. 'No one else was willing… You understand?'

Georgie's mother nodded her head.

'He was our... how do you say? Black sheep?' Catalena asked.

The other ladies murmured agreement.

'But he was still my brother, and when I was little I loved him...'

'I loved him too,' Joyce said. 'For a while...'

And Georgie watched as Catalena rose and embraced her mother, the two of them with tears in their eyes.

'And this is Hugo's granny, from Canada,' Georgie's granny said.

The older lady smiled and said in her soft warm voice, 'I'm very happy to meet you.'

Georgie liked her at once. 'Me too. Hugo is my favouritest person in all the world!' she said, then glanced at her mother and grandmother. 'After Mummy and Granny and my little brother...'

The ladies laughed.

'I'm glad,' Hugo's granny said. She exchanged a look with the other ladies. 'And he's probably my favouritest person in all the world... now that his father is dead. I'm hoping he'll be willing to come back to Canada with me and complete his education there.' She looked around at the others. 'There's nothing for him here.'

'Georgie, darling, will you just go and check on Robbie, please,' her mother requested. 'Then perhaps you'd like to play in your room?'

Georgie smothered her rebellion. They were obviously going to start talking about the interesting things now and wanted her out of the way.

'Yes, Mummy,' she said and left the room, leaving the door slightly ajar behind her. She scampered loudly upstairs to check on Robbie, talking loudly as if he could understand. Then when she reckoned she had done her task, she crept back downstairs to her place on the stairs. If she listened hard maybe she could hear what they were saying.

CHAPTER 74

'I am sorry,' Catalena was saying. 'This is all my brother's fault. Wherever he went, he caused big troubles.'

Georgie listened hard.

'From the moment my father married his mother, Jorge set out to make trouble. But my father was not willing to be defeated by a child. Once my brothers and I arrived, he had Jorge sent to a boarding school in Buenos Aires while we remained at the hacienda on the pampas.

'But Jorge was expelled. My father tried to interest him in the family business but he seemed to prefer to consort with the city low-life. Finally he was sent to Chicago where my father had business interests – but there again, Jorge seemed to take pleasure in doing what would most shame his family.'

Catalena cast a swift glance at Joyce.

'I don't know how much of this you know?'

Joyce spread her hands wide. 'Very little. He arrived here as the son of a wealthy local landowner looking to inherit a castle or two.' She smiled ruefully. 'And he discovered his father had simply made it all up to impress a young lady and her family back in Buenos Aires.'

'Ah yes,' Catalena said, with a sigh. 'It is so. We children used to mock him for clinging to these fantasies, but he was determined.' She paused then asked bluntly, 'Did you know he had been to prison?'

Joyce gasped. 'No! What happened? What did he do?'

'In Chicago it amused him to sideline as a driver for the Capone gang – driving illicit whisky, helping with protection rackets, things like that. When Capone was sent to prison, so were his gang members. I don't know if you knew how many were Scots? It was said Al Capone only trusted his Scots bodyguards.'

'And George worked for him?' Hannah asked.

Catalena nodded. 'And so he was rounded up with the others and imprisoned. Then at the end of their sentence, because he had a Scottish surname, Jorge was deported with them back to Scotland.'

'Ah, so that's why he was in Glasgow,' Joyce said, suddenly understanding. 'With gang members from Glasgow.' She nodded. 'I see.'

Hannah added, 'I remember there was a crackdown on gangs in Glasgow. It was in all the newspapers – and then George turned up here in search of his fortune.'

Mother and daughter exchanged glances.

'That fits,' Joyce said.

'You said he was involved in illegal alcohol running in Chicago?' Hannah asked.

Catalena nodded.

'I wonder,' Hannah said thoughtfully. 'I wonder was that why he was so keen to get his hands on a car or two – so he could do the same thing here? Wick, you see, is dry, like Chicago,' she explained to Catalena. 'There would be opportunities for a man of his experience.'

'I wouldn't be surprised,' Catalena said. 'I am so very sorry.'

'It is probably better that we didn't know – that we don't know,' Hannah said firmly. 'Now that he is gone…'

'We have a chance of a fresh start,' Joyce said. Her voice was quiet but determined. 'For me and my family.'

'Well done.' It was the soft Canadian voice of Hugo's granny. 'It sounds as though he was as bad a man as his father was.' Nancy looked across at Hannah. 'I knew Geordie Sinclair and he was bad through and through.'

'In the Klondike?' Hannah asked quietly.

Nancy looked surprised. 'Yes. He was there with Hugh's father.'

'Hughie Mackay,' Hannah put in.

'Yes.'

'Hughie was engaged to my sister, Belle,' Hannah said.

Nancy's eyes widened. 'Ah. And it was Belle who wrote to Hughie and sent back the Mizpah ring.' She paused. 'Where is it now? I gave it to Hugh when he married… his first wife, Katie. She died of cancer when Hugo was quite young.'

'Hugh gave it to Ruby…' Joyce began.

'The girl who was killed in the accident?' Nancy asked.

'Yes.'

'Ah. So maybe it is lost…' said Nancy. 'And maybe that's for the best. If Belle had not sent back the ring, Hughie would never have known Geordie had betrayed him. They would never have fought and Hughie would not have been killed.'

She sighed. 'But then again, I wouldn't have got away from the Klondike and found myself welcomed by Bill and Marie Alexander.' She smiled at her listeners and explained. 'Hughie's aunt and uncle. They were lovely people – genuine, good-hearted Christian people who took me in and helped me, even when they knew the whole story. Geordie had frightened me into pretending he was Hughie, but it all came out and Bill Alexander sent him away.'

She looked across at Catalena sadly. 'He must have made his way to Buenos Aires…'

'He met my mother's brother in San Francisco and came home with him. He inveigled himself into the family and married my mother – she was very young!' Catalena added.

'So what happened to Geordie?' Nancy asked.

'He was killed. Shot in a poker game. His opponent thought he was cheating,' Catalena said.

'And he probably was,' Nancy said. She sighed. 'So now father and son have gone. We must pray that their bad blood has gone with them.' She looked around. 'We do get second chances. I know that.' She smiled. 'Marie Alexander led me to faith in her Lord Jesus and that has made all the difference in my life. Through the Alexanders I met and married my beloved Clem. He was our local pastor and a truly good man. "Everyone deserves a fresh start" he used to say. He refused to hold anyone's past against them, once they had taken that step into new life. So maybe once we get these funerals over, we can begin again – as Joyce said. Maybe a new generation can do better than the old?'

CHAPTER 75

Georgie had got bored sitting on the stairs straining to keep up with the grown-ups' conversation. She did not really understand it. So many names and people and old stories. She stretched and wriggled a bit. Then she had an idea.

Hesitantly she pushed the sitting-room door open and caught her mother's eye.

'I'd like to go out to play,' Georgie said. 'For a little while. In the garden. It's not raining.'

She did not really want to play by herself, but Amanda had gone to live with her granny out in the country. She missed Amanda.

She did have her new little brother Robbie to play with. But she could not take him outside to play because he was too small. He was very nice and he liked cuddles and he had a lovely smile. Georgie liked the way he held on to her finger. Yes, a brother was a good thing. Though maybe she would have liked a puppy or a kitten better.

'Please can I go out to play?' she asked. 'I'll be good.'

The grown-ups, interrupted in their important conversation, shooed her away as she hoped they would. She skipped out of the door and down the path to where the garden was nice and wild. She thought she might try climbing the gnarly old tree that was nearly hidden by tall weeds. As she reached for a foothold, she spotted Hugo approaching from the pathway along the clifftop.

'Hugo! Hugo!' she waved excitedly.

To her dismay he scowled at her. 'What are you doing here? You shouldn't be out on your own...'

'I'm not,' Georgie crowed. 'You're here now!'

But it didn't make him laugh. In fact, if he was not a boy, and quite a grown-up one at that, she might have thought he had been crying. She clambered down from the tree and ran to join him.

'There's ladies in our house,' she told him importantly. 'And one of them's your granny. I've met her. She's very nice.'

But Hugo did not seem to want to talk.

'Are you coming in?' she asked. 'There's tea and cakes and...'

He stopped still, then turned to glare down at her. She froze at the expression on his face. She had never seen him anything but smiley and friendly and kind. Now, he looked... angry with her. But how could that be? Had she done wrong?

Suddenly she felt frightened. Would Hugo punish her? She knew bad girls had to be punished. She remembered her daddy saying that. And it was horrible and it made you cry.

'Tea and cakes and people visiting?' Hugo demanded. 'And it's all lovely. That's what you think, don't you?' And suddenly, unbelievably, he was shouting at her. 'Well it's not. It's horrible. My dad's dead and I'm going to have to go to his funeral and that's all wrong and he shouldn't be dead...'

'My dad's dead too,' Georgie said softly, trying to comfort him. She reached up her hand to slip it into his, but he pushed her away.

'Good riddance to him!' he shouted.

'Hugo!' Georgie protested in horror. 'You can't say that!'

'Oh yes I can.' Hugo glared at her. 'Because it's all your dad's fault! Everything's his fault! He killed my dad! Your dad is the worst person in the whole world. George St Clair! George Sinclair!' Hugo spat the name out. 'I hate him, I hate him, I hate him! I never want to hear that name again. George Sinclair! I'll hate that name till the day I die!'

And he turned and stormed off back down the path.

Georgie stood where he had left her, his angry hurting words scorching into her brain. A flurry of rain suddenly came out of nowhere and she took to her heels.

Breathlessly she ran up the garden path. Opening the house door, she listened carefully. The quiet murmur of grown-up voices continued from the sitting room. She hung up her coat carefully, then opened the sitting-room door. Four heads turned to look at her.

'Georgie,' her mother said.

'Georgie,' her grandmother said.

Georgie… George…

Hugo's voice pounded in her head. 'George Sinclair! I never want to hear that name again. I'll hate that name till the day I die.'

Georgie announced quietly, 'I don't want to be called Georgie any more.' She looked at her mother and grandmother and the two ladies sitting there. 'Please don't call me Georgie any more.'

'But why, darling?' her mother asked.

'Because of Daddy,' Georgie whispered, tears in her eyes. 'Hugo says he hates the name George…'

The women exchanged glances.

'So what shall we call you?' her grandmother asked her gently.

Georgie puzzled about that for a minute, then she said, 'I know. I've got a middle name. Belle. I'll be Belle from now on.'

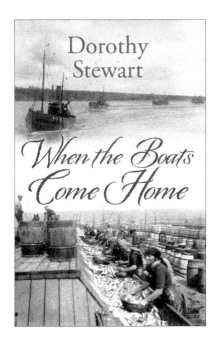

WHEN THE BOATS
COME HOME

DOROTHY STEWART

A Christian novel about family secrets, romance and revival in a
1921 fishing town.

October 1921 and the herring fishing fleets have converged on
Great Yarmouth for the autumn season. Wick fisherman Robbie
Ross has come to blows with his father and been thrown off
the family boat. His sister, war widow Lydia, reluctantly sets out
to bring him home, little knowing her world and her family are
about to be turned upside down.

Paperback 368pp, ISBN 9781909824676
Available on Kindle

THE MIZPAH RING

DOROTHY STEWART

Book One of the Mizpah Ring Trilogy

'I wouldn't marry you if you were the last man on earth!'

And so Belle Reid sets in train three generations of heartbreak and sorrow, death and disaster.

Geordie, her spurned suitor, sets out from Wick to make his fortune in the Klondike gold rush of 1897 – but his ticket to that fortune depends on the rival Belle has chosen over him. When the lads find gold, and rival Hughie has the Mizpah ring made to send to Belle, it's time for Geordie to make his move – and only one of them can win.

Paperback 322pp, ISBN 9781909824997
Available on Kindle